Richard Harris

Mayfair to Millbank

A novel. Part 2

Richard Harris

Mayfair to Millbank
A novel. Part 2

ISBN/EAN: 9783337065195

Printed in Europe, USA, Canada, Australia, Japan

Cover: Foto ©Andreas Hilbeck / pixelio.de

More available books at **www.hansebooks.com**

MAYFAIR TO MILLBANK.

A NOVEL.

IN THREE VOLUMES.

BY

RICHARD HARRIS,

Author of " New Nobility," &c.

VOL. II.

London:

T. CAUTLEY NEWBY, PUBLISHER,
30, WELBECK STREET, CAVENDISH SQUARE.
1870.

MAYFAIR TO MILLBANK.

CHAPTER I.

GIPSY GUIDES.

EDGAR had advanced only a few steps from the tents, when, turning himself without appearing to notice the movements of the gipsies, he perceived them engaged in a sharp controversy; the subject of it, he believed was himself; their countenances, as the blazing fire shone upon them, manifested great excitement, and evidently the propriety of accompanying their guest on his

disagreeable journey was the matter of debate.
The woman with the fiendish countenance was
endeavouring to dissuade the tall gipsy from
his voluntarily imposed task. Bill stood with his
hands thrust into his pockets, and occasionally
expectorated into the fire, taking no further part
in the dispute than that of listener. Their language was less intelligible than their looks and
gestures, but these were sufficiently violent to
excite no little apprehension in the mind of the
traveller. But if any doubt had remained as to
the subject of their conference the words of the
dark woman as she caught the half turned figure
of Edgar, through the partially illumined gloom,
would have dispelled it instantly.

"D'ye see he's listening?" said she.

Edgar turned away, and an involuntary shudder passed through his frame.

"Come on, Bill," said the tall gipsy.

"May the devil's shirt collar reward ye for a
fool," said the woman. "Toby, Tib, d'ye hear—
there wake up ye sleepy dogs, and if the gentle-

man must be protected, do ye all lend a han', d'ye hear?"

"Come on, come on," said Bill, "the sooner to it the sooner over."

"Get ready, Sue, for starting by the glimmer o' daybreak."

"Ye'll not be back by daylight, Sam, mark me."

"Devil mark ye," said Sam; "come on, Bill."

Thus saying, the two followed Edgar, who had withdrawn some little distance when he saw that he was observed listening to the conversation. Meanwhile, he had carefully adjusted a pair of pistols, which he had concealed in his breast pocket, so as to be more accessible in case of emergency; for he felt that the persons who were to be his guard were about the most formidable that could be selected from all that villainous group. Indeed, if danger were to be apprehended from a journey over so wild a tract it could only be from such as those who were forcing their company upon him.

They proceeded for some distance in silence, for Edgar's mind was too busy to permit him for awhile to open a conversation which he felt would be little more than an effort of courtesy ; however, even this was deemed at last the better policy, as he would be the more likely by that means to obtain an insight into the character, if not the intentions, of his protectors.

" I suppose," said he, " you know these parts well ?"

" For that, master," answered the gipsy, " there ain't many parts o' England as we don't know."

" Then you have no need of maps," said Edgar, " to show you the way ?"

"Maps, sir ?"

" Oh, I see," continued Edgar, " I mean paper with all the roads marked on it."

" He means them pickter things," said Bill.

" Lor bless yer honor, there ain't no road but what we could tell yer how many milestones there be between the furdest on 'em an Lunnun."

"How far is it to—to—Heathmoor?" asked Edgar.

"Heathmoor, is it yer honor wants?" said Tim.

"I don't say I want it," answered Edgar, "but if you tell me how far it is to Heathmoor I shall know about the distance to the place I am going to."

"Well, it's nothing to us, yer honor, where you're going; but Heathmoor, I s'pose, is about fourteen mile, or thereaways. It's an old place that, and arnted, they says."

"So I have heard," replied Edgar, "and I mean to go and see it if I can. No one lives there, I believe."

"No one did live there but a old ooman, sir, but o' late somebody else av come to it, and the old ooman av bin turned out."

"When might that have been?" asked Edgar.

"Within a week or so," said the gipsy.

"Are you sure."

"Sure enough," said Sam. "She wur a good old crittur, she wur, and it's a mortal shame she wur packed off; but these gentry, yer honor, will do as they likes, and the devil can't stop 'em."

"Are you sure you are not mistaken?" asked Edgar, with too much apprehension that it was true.

"It's right enough.   They says as how the right owner's come in for it at last, else it wasn't nobody's by rights, they says."

"Do you know who it is," asked Edgar.

"Squire Hindly, they says, that lives away down at Raymond's Park, and sends old women to prison for pickin' up sticks."

An imprecation or two, conveyed in the mild language of an oath which would have almost shocked Satan himself, followed this speech.

"And did you know the old housekeeper?"

"Knowed her well; both her and the one as was there afore her."

"Her name?"

"Wilmerton! I bleeve," answered Sam.

"Wilmonton!" said Tim.

"Well, some called her one and some t'other,"

said Sam, "but that was near enough for us. She'd allays a basin o' good soup or a cup a beer for a hard-up traveller, *that* I knows."

The surprise of Edgar was concealed by the darkness of the night; but his tone and manner were hardly so much disguised. He was relieved to a great extent from that horrible apprehension which he had experienced at starting, as the conversation of his companions evinced that, in spite of their exterior roughness, they possessed some of the better feelings of human nature; that they were susceptible of gratitude, and capable of being wrought upon by kindness. So far, then, he felt that he had a better weapon at his command than the pistols which pressed against his bosom.

"And what became of this Wilmington?"

"That's the krect word, sir," said Tim, "that's it."

"You're right, Tim," replied Sam. "What become of her, sir, why that I raly don't know, for the last time I called there they let the dog at me—d'ye mind, Tim?"

"Egad," said Tim, " I've got cause to mind it, sure enough. I shall carry the mark o' that bite to my grave."

"That was kind," said Edgar, "they might have treated you civilly."

" Ah !" said the gipsy, "you see, master, them as has to rough the world meets about as much pity as there be in a wolf's mouth. I never fell out with my lot yet, and never means to. We've got as many acres as the biggest lord, ain't us, Bill ?"

" We have so," said Bill.

" But, it's my bleef," continued Tim, " that if these gentryfied fellers could shut out the sun from us they'd 'ave all the daylight to theirselves."

" I think," said Edgar, "you blame all for a few ; I will grant that there are many of these avaricious men who, while they look upon themselves as little less than gods, regard their fellow creatures as little more than brutes."

" Some on us had better bin horses," said Bill.

" I wish I'd bin a 'orse," said Tim, limping, ''when that dog was at my eels."

"Yer see, sir, there's one thing as I prides myself on in this 'ere world, and it's the pride o'our whole tribe; you laughs at pride, I dis say, but it's true; and that 'ere is, that we won't serve a livin' soul; they can drive us from common to common, but they can't make us work for 'em; can 'em, Bill?"

"No," said Bill, spitting furiously through his teeth, and thrusting his hands still deeper into his pockets till his elbows were almost buried.

"But, you see," said Edgar, "you have less to complain of than most men. The greater number of us are in some way or other subservient to the will of others—that is, most men have masters— you acknowledge none—therefore you are most free."

"Yes," said Tim, "but we ain't to be 'unted down like foxes with dorgs, ay, Bill?"

Bill shook his head, and uttered a dreadful oath.

"You see, sir, you're a gent," said Sam, "and in course has their feelins'; 'hap you got plenty without seekin' it, and God bless yer honor with it. I wish there was more o' your sort, I do; but why should a man, 'cause he's got a 'undred acres, kick a poor devil 'cause he's got none, as though he was a weed under his foot that ought to be hucked up—that's the way to put it, sir. My poor old mother as was turned eighty was sent to prison last buthday but one for picking up a turmut—poor crittur, it was a 'ard buthday that, to live to eighty, and spend it in jail, for such a thing as that—by G—d, sir, if there's a God there'll be a pay day—poor old crittur!"

Edgar could not but sympathize with the honest feeling of the gipsy; but being desirous for more reasons than one, to divert the conversation, he endeavoured to turn it again into the channel which was more to his purpose.

"But you see," said he, "you who owe no allegiance to the class you speak of, that is, you who are independent of the gentry, are not the only persons who are treated harshly by them; this poor old mistress Wilmington, you say, was turned adrift without notice, and probably without

any means of support, perhaps no home to go to.
Had she a family ?"

"I bleeve there was a gal, but I dunnow."

"Yes, yes," said Bill, "the young ooman as
Peggy said dandled her bairn."

"Wor she the darter?" said Tim.

"Sure enough ; and as putty a wench as ever
lived."

"Did she live with the housekeeper ?" enquired
Edgar.

"I've seen her there about a year and a half
or so ago," answered Bill ; " but what come on
her arter that, the Lord knows. My old ooman
allays used to ask about her, for she wor a nice
creature, she wor ; but I rather bleeve she married, now I come to think."

Those who have fondly loved may imagine
Edgar's feelings at this announcement. Although
anxious to push his inquiries, he feared to betray
too much of the interest which he felt, and for
awhile he wrestled with a host of conflicting feelings which were aroused by the last remark. It

seemed impossible to be true. Lizzy could not have married; her promise bound her to him; and, in spite of any counteracting influences which he knew had been exerted to lure her from him, he believed that her own affection was superior to them all. It was true she had written to him to say that she dared no longer hope, that her heart was well nigh broken with the misery that she had been the unhappy cause of inflicting upon his family; but that was rather a confirmation of her affection than a token of estrangement. But what made his veins tingle as he heard the remark? what sent that thrill through his heart? His whole life, past and future, seemed to be in the scale against that moment, but that little moment weighed down all.

" How far are we from the inn you spoke of ?" he inquired, after a long pause.

" You see that ere light glimmering over the brow there ?" said Sam.

No, Edgar could not see it—his eyes seemed to swim.

" Down there yonder," said the gipsy, pointing towards the dark horizon.

" By the side of that clump," said Tim.

" I see it now."

" That's it; but it's a long way off yet—three mile and more."

" But now here's the road," said Sam, " an' if yer keep as straight as yer can goo, yer can't miss it."

" I'd tell your honour to keep a sharp look out both sides o' the way," said Bill.

" Is there danger of being stopped ?" inquired Edgar, somewhat alarmed at this premonitory remark.

" Well, you see this here's the turnpike ; and to tell yer the plain truth, forewarned 'ere and forearmed aint bad things. What wi' game-keepers and—"

" Hold yer dam tongue, Bill," said Tim ; " do yer think a gamekeeper 'ud rob a genleman ?"

The fear of gamekeepers to the poacher is about as natural as that of highwaymen to the

traveller, and therefore it was somewhat excusable if Bill's dread for his natural enemy peeped
out for a moment from behind his habitual
cunning.

"Howsomever," added Bill, "keep your eyes
open, sir, and if a chap asks yer for a skiver, use
him like a Christian."

"If he asks me for gold I'll give him lead,"
said Edgar, smiling, "though I should be loth
to harm a fellow if I could avoid it."

"God bless you, sir," said Sam, "and cuss the
chap as harms you. If I thought there was any
fear, I'd go with yer to the public; but I knows
yer all right. If all folks was as good as you, we
should be a deal better."

"Hush!" exclaimed Tim, "here be the
coach."

"So she be," said Bill, "Now, sir, you be all
right. She'll be here in less nor no time."

Edgar listened; but to his ear all was silent.
Not a sound broke the stillness in which nature
was hushed, for the wind, which in the early

evening had presaged a tempest, had now died away into an unbroken calm, and the night shone out brilliant and dazzling with the hoar frost glittering on every spray.

"I don't hear it," said Edgar.

"Now," said Sam, "she's a comin' over the gravelled road the tother side o' the hill; you'll hear her now an agin, as she comes up the brow."

Tim spoke truly, for the rattling of wheels was just audible as they listened; and after gaining the summit of the hill, the welcome trot of four horses could be distinctly heard.

"We must say ' good-night,' sir," said Tim.

"Stay, my good fellows," said Edgar; "your kindness must have something more than thanks. Here's a trifle to make your hearts merry round your evening fire."

"The Lord bless yer 'onour," said the gipsies; "and if ever Sam Lee " ("or Bill Cooper," said the other) "can sarve yer, he's your man. We be rough 'uns, but smoothlike's no manner o' use to we who've got a rough world to dale with. Good-night 'ee, sir—good-night."

Thus saying, the gipsies took their leave and retraced their steps over the lonely moor.

Meanwhile the coach had come up, and Edgar was soon seated on its top and hastening towards the inn, whose bright light became more and more distinct until the welcome blaze of the huge log that lay crackling in the fire-place of its principal chamber, inspired the travellers with the anticipation of good cheer and lively gossip.

CHAPTER II.

A ROADSIDE INN.

THE roadside inns of thirty years ago are fast fading from remembrance. There are men who still delight to recall the reminiscences of the coach times; of the three days journey on the outside; of the lively canter down hill; of the keen north-easter setting across a certain marsh; of the being fixed in, and the being dug out of the snow; and above all of mine host, with the rosy face, as cheerful as his blazing fire, and the well served repast, and the fireside legend. Those were days and scenes that England will never

know again. Never was effected such a social trans-
formation as when steam sent her whistle through
wood and field.   Poetry uttered her last " wood
note wild," and bade farewell to a land where
there were none to listen to her strains. Methinks
the singing birds must soon follow, for even these
will not care to warble to ears that are only
awakened by the clamour of the market-place or
the shrieking of a railway engine.   Poet, I commend your courage, I admire your song, but I
deplore the coldness of your audience.

The " Talbot " was an ancient inn, of goodly
appearance for the locality in which it was
situated, and of dimensions which told of the
prosperity of other days. It stood in the midst
of a wild and desolate region, such as I have
before attempted to describe.   Immediately in
front, and separated only by the branch road
which diverged a little from the turnpike, was a
large pond, the immense expanse of which might
almost have won for it the title of lake ; on either
side of the inn were the coach houses and stables,

with their rustic covering of thatch, while in the rear of all were the large garden and orchard, well stocked with fruit trees, and ornamented with such fantastic archways, arbours, and seats, as the worthy host, in the fertility of his morning brain, could devise.

As the coach "pulled up," the usual bustle ensued, and the travellers were conducted to the public room by the landlord, who received orders and transmitted them, pulled the heavy, half-consumed log round, so as to produce a more cheerful blaze, and called out lustily for another faggot. In a few minutes the table was smoking with boiled and roast, and with vegetables in goodly profusion, at which Edgar tood his seat with the rest of the company. After the substantial repast was finished, there followed the grog and tobacco, and in little less than an hour after their arrival, the company was as much at home with itself as though the oldest acquaint-ances had met after years of separation; the irrepressible parish clerk, with other official and

local dignitaries, having dropped in for their
wonted potations, which they swallowed with the
usual compound of the latest news.

The recent proceedings at Heathmoor having
formed the subject of village wonderment for the
last ten days, were a still fresh and welcome
topic of conversation among those who claimed
connection with the neighbourhood.   Butcher
and baker were anxious for its occupation by a
good family ; nor was the clerk or beadle less so,
since the former, in addition to his ecclesiastical
preferment, amused his leisure hours in making
clothes, and the latter in manufacturing boots.
The landlord drew forth his " churchwarden pipe"
from the rustling heap, and, after sundry preparatory blows down the stem, commenced the
business of filling.   Much discursive conversation followed, and the news which the travellers brought, having been recounted, the
subject of so much speculation was about to be
introduced by the clerk, when a little diminutive
gentleman, who turned his head very much up as

he surveyed the company through a pair of green spectacles, inquired if Heathmoor was very far from the inn.

The clerk checked himself instantly. Mr. Sawbury, the butcher, hemmed, like one preparing to listen to an interesting address, while the beadle made ready by sonorously blowing his nose, which organ being of very powerful magnitude, startled the company into profound silence for the next minute.

"The distance," said the landlord, to whom the question had been addressed, "be about a mile."

"Mile and a quarter, *I* call it," said the clerk.

"You can't do it much under," added Sawbury, in a very gentle manner; "but if you are going up, sir, I can give you a lift, for I am agoing thereabouts."

"The gentleman stops here to-night," said the landlord; "leastways, I think I understood you to say so, sir."

The little gentleman bowed his head in a very dignified and precise manner, and then swallowed his gin and water.

"Fine mansion, sir," said the clerk, finding that the inquirer seemed in no ways inclined to continue the subject, and determined, if possible, to ascertain if any of the strangers were connected with the place.

"Pity it ain't let," added the beadle; "it wur a good family that wur there last. I s'pose *I* served 'em," he added, leaning a little over his shoulder towards the person who sat next to him, "forty pair o' boots a year, 'sides slippers and so on."

"Be it let, sir, might I ask?" inquired Hopkins.

"I believe not," answered the gentleman, "I *believe* not."

"There has bin tales that the rightful heir be come to it lately," said Hopkins.

"Indeed!" said the traveller. "Was it sometime then in doubt as to that?"

"Well, I bleeve there wur some query about the title," replied Hopkins; "leastways so the tale went; but you know we village folks never hardly gets to the rights o' things, tho' we lives close by; but I dissay, sir, you have heard as well as us, that the son of a certain squire, away down at—lor, what's the name?—bless my soul."

"Raymonds," said Sawbury. "I knows the place well, and Squire Hindly too, and the son likewise—knows 'em as well as I knows you."

"That's the name," said Hopkins. "But I wur a going to say, I bleeve this son turned out wildish—leastways, that's as we hears; but you know I don't put much faith in these ere ear-says, I don't; and I hope it warn't true, for the lady I'm sure were as nice a crittur as ever trod in shoe leather. Be it true, sir, she's lately dead?"

"I am sorry to say it is," answered the stranger; "poor thing, I believe her heart was fairly broke."

"Deed," said Hopkins; "and how were that, sir, might I be 'lowed to ask?"

The little gentleman shook his head, but said nothing in reply, contenting himself with the importance which his silence secured him.

"I thought there were something in it," said the clerk; "it was a deuced pretty girl that were living there, though."

"Do you think as that was her?" asked the beadle.

A smile went round the company, and that cunning demeanour which is common to persons in subservient positions, when enjoying the pastime of maligning their superiors, was exhibited; while each urged his neighbour to utter sentiments which he feared to avow himself.

Edgar, though writhing under the torture which the conversation inflicted, preserved an appearance of calmness and good humour which was so necessary for the purpose of unriddling the whole matter. As he plainly perceived that neither the boastful butcher, nor the strange gentleman, in whatever manner he might be connected with Heathmoor, could entertain the slightest suspicion as to himself, he ventured to stimulate the conversation by enquiring if the subject which afforded so much amusement was a love adventure; taking care at the same time to treat the matter with so much levity as might throw the most crafty off his guard.

" Something of the sort, sir," answered Hopkins; " but I bleeve both the gentleman and the girl were made much worse of than they deserved. Suppose the young feller were a bit wild, there ain't so much harm in sowing your wild oats as there be in keeping 'em in stock. Out wi 'em, says I; it all makes good for trade, though I'll grant yer it ain't the best o' farming nuther."

" I think the young woman's mother were worse than the daughter," said the clerk; " she ought not to have hencouraged it; but hi believe she were a queer crechure herself, by hall haccount."

"The mystery is," said Sawbury, "how the doose they comed here? the last place of all I should 'ave thought for 'em to take to."

"The pride of girls now-a-days is," said the stranger, "that many of them would rather be gentlemen's mistresses than working men's wives."

"That's true—that's true," said a chorus of voices.

"The old Squire were too harsh," said the host; "he might ha done it all in a more gentler way.   And it's my bleef that there were nothing wrong about the whole thing, any further than the young genleman wanted to marry up to her."

"Likely!" exclaimed the clerk; "his it likely now that a gentleman would marry ha poor girl like that just because she ad a pretty face? Why, how long do it last?"

"Yours didn't last long anyhow!" said Sawbury, who was by no means on the best of terms with the clerk; some little quarrel at the last vestry having severed their friendship, in spite of their oft repeated toast about "difference of opinion," &c., &c.

"It wernt painted with bullock's blood any how," murmured the clerk, rather aside.

"At any rate," said the jocund Boniface, "it ain't well for us to run down the young gentleman, though he were, as I've heard, turned out o' doors by the Squire; for it's my bleef that he'll come here and live; and if so be he do, a gentleman who spends his money like a prince, and 'as a 'art as big as his fortun', is just the neighbour as we wants. Now, I think you've heard me say as how I lived with the fam'ly of the Mortons, which was as good a faml'y p'raps as ever was, and if I ain't mistaken, this 'ere lady that the gentleman says is lately dead, Heaven bless her—I say, if I ain't werry much mistaken, this 'ere lady were a daughter of the old baronet, my master."

There was a pause, while Hopkins wetted his
lips with half a tumbler of gin and water, an
example which was speedily followed by several
of the others ; the beadle, meanwhile, taking
advantage of the interval to sound once more his
sonorous double barrel organ.

There was a great rattling of spoons and glasses
as the tumblers were returned to the table, and
Hopkins again proceeded.

"You see, neighbours, I think I told you I
lived with the Mortons, and, if I ain't mistaken,
the werry property of Heathmoor were the matter
of a lawsuit, or something, while I were in the
family. Miss Mortons were then a young lady
—gal, I may call her, risin' seven. Now,
I minds hearin' the old genleman say that he ,
meant the property, in case he winned the lawsuit, for this ere little Ellie ; I left soon after, and
I think I been landlord o' the 'Talbot' werry near
ever since. Now, in case Mrs. Hindly did comed
in for it, nothing are more likely than this young
scapegrace, as you calls him, should have it at
her death ?"

"Good!" said the clerk, who, having once been errand boy in a lawyer's office, was generally looked up to as an indisputable authority on all questions involving legal difficulties, and was the chief arbiter in all local disputes, excepting those which required magisterial interference.

"It would go by heirship," said he; "especially if it were left never to be sold."

"And may that be?" enquired Edgar.

"Course," said the clerk; "a man may leave his property as he likes. Why, to prove that, I made Farmer Giles will t'other day, and he left his houses so as they *can't* be sold—from father to son, from father to son, and so on for ever."

"That be right enough," said the beadle, "for *I* signed the will."

"Then this young gentleman must come in for it," said Hopkins; "and if he be anything like un's grandfather, he be a damned good feller."

"But excuse me, Mr. —, I beg your pardon," said the gentleman, addressing the clerk.

"Smith my name is, sir."

"Mr. Smith, but you know—at least, I suppose, you know there is such a thing as tenancy by the curtesey of England?"

Mr. Smith drew his pipe from his mouth and partially concealed the astonishment which beamed from his grey dew-drop looking eyes, by the dense cloud of smoke which he purposely whiffed forth. Meanwhile, all eyes were turned upon the village lawyer, anxiously watching to see in what way his legal erudition would display itself, or whether he were really posed by the strange gentleman; Sawbury, above all, hoping that his ignorance would utterly confound him.

"Well, you see," said he, "hit hall depends upon the will, hi think you said, Hopkins, that it were left to this lady's son?"

"I didn't say no such thing," answered the host, "and I don't pertend to know no more o' the matter than I said."

"You ain't answered the gentleman's question, Smith," said Sawbury, with a broad grin. "Mr.

Smith didn't erzackly understand you, sir," he added, addressing the little gentleman in the corner, who was quietly enjoying the proceedings.

"I beg your parding, Mr. Sawbury, hi did hunderstand perfectly well, and it were best for those who don't hunderstand to hold their tongues."

"I'll bet glasses round as you *don't* understand the question as was put to you."

"Solomon says that—"

"We don't want Solomon," said Sawbury, "when we've got such men as you—hold your tongue, Smith, or you'll never get another will to make."

"For my own part," said Hopkins, whose business it was to preserve the good humour of his guests and prevent any further disputations amongst them than served to further the evening's amusement, "for my own part I'm as igorant o' the law as a beer barrel, and if all men settled their quarrels with a comfortable glass of grog, lawyers' bills and sparrows' bills would be about the same length. May I take the liberty to ask, sir, if the spression you used meant a bad title in the young man, or is what we calls in plain English a morgidge?"

It was impossible to preserve a countenance free from a smile at the frank simplicity of the honest innkeeper, and as the little gentleman laughed, so did little Mr. Smith, who knew that a laugh under the circumstances would rather redound to his credit than confirm his ignorance.

"It simply means, my worthy friend," said the gentleman, "that the husband is entitled to the wife's lands as long as he lives."

"Erzactly," said Smith, "to the housting of the hare of course, and so the Squire comes hin before the son."

"You're like my Dimond," said Sawbury, referring to a well-known horse of his, "an' he goes like anything in the sharps, but jibs like a hass in trace harness. You was born to say ' amen,' Smith, and so long as you sticks to that it don't matter where the text is."

" I tell you what, Sawbury, if it warn't for my place, hi'd make you pray for mercy before hi said hamen ! "

" I say, Smith, don't, for the sake of your place. You knows at the last westry it was said as how you drawled too much, and had too much of the methodist style for the church; it wouldn't be the thing you know to go into your desk next Sunday wi' two black eyes."

" And it wouldn't sound well at the bench, next license day, for it to be said that thic black eyes were got at the ' Talbot,' neighbours ; so let's drink a toast to the next tenant of Heathmoor, whether it's our friend here by the ingle or the young gentleman as I believe will come to it one day."

" Hear, hear," cried the unanimous voices of the company, while the little gentleman rose to thank them so far as he was concerned in the matter, assuring them that so far from his being the tenant, he was only there on a matter of busi-

o 5

ness, but he heartily joined them, nevertheless, in their good wishes towards the Squire's son.

Great cheering followed the neat little speech of the gentleman with the spectacles, for the grog was telling well among the company, and soon had the usual effect of promoting, if not harmony at least an unmusical discord, which is generally a sign of concord. In due time the company separated, and Edgar retired to his chamber to reflect upon the strange incidents which had taken place during that eventful day.

CHAPTER III.

BOBBIE'S SECRET.

AFTER partaking of a substantial breakfast on the following morning, Edgar strolled into the well ordered garden of the 'Talbot,' where he found the worthy landlord occupied in training some choice espaliers.

"You have a fine garden, landlord," remarked the young man.

"Good mornin, sir," said Hopkins, touching his hat, and stepping from the border on which he had been employed. "I wur not aware, sir,

but you were going by the first coach, or I should
not a called you so early ; it's a nice bracin' air,
sir, aint it ? "

" I shall probably remain with you another
night," answered Edgar.

The landlord, with the curiosity of his calling,
was immediately on our friend's trail : there was
no doubt then, that his business also, was in some
way connected with Heathmoor, but, if so, how
stood the conversation of the previous night?

" Very happy sir, to make you comfortable.
Hope you slept well, sir; our customers are a
werry mixed lot, and our neighbours such as you
saw last night, are generly o' the same turn—
chaff you know, sir, and the talk o' the place and
so on, wi' market ncos once a week and every
month the westry."

" But last night," said Fdgar, " they seemed
to have something of a different sort to discuss—
this Heathmoor seems to be a place of some
note."

" Well, sir, so it be as far as that goes. You see

it's the only house like in the place you may say, and it's been empty a good bit, and nobody knows what to make of it,—but may be, sir, you know more about un than I do."

"In that case," said Edgar, "I should have no curiosity to satisfy by questioning you on the subject. May I ask who were the persons referred to as the beautiful girl, and the mother?"

"Oh, that were Mrs. Wilmington and her gal what lived there awhile."

"The housekeeper?" I suppose.

"Well, not erzactly," said Hopkins, smiling, and at the same time scanning the features of Edgar with the keenest scrutiny. "But pardon me, sir, might I make a guess?"

"Guess!" said Edgar, "you have a right to guess without my leave. What do you guess, Hopkins?"

"That you be Mr. Hindly."

"What leads you to such a conclusion?" asked Edgar, astonished at his being recognized.

"As soon as you spoked I thought I knowed

the voice.   You heard I say as how I lived wi'
your grandfather?"

"I believe you said you were in the service of
Sir George Morton."

"I were," added the landlord, "and the more
I looks at you the more certain I be that you be
his grandson."

"I confess, my good friend," said Edgar,
"that you are not far from correct; but keep the
matter secret.   It is as you have guessed; and
now tell me something about Heathmoor and—"

"I will," exclaimed the landlord, taking the
proffered hand of the young gentleman, and
joyous at the thought of meeting a member of
the family with which so many agreeable asso-
ciations were connected.   "You know, sir, I
married my wife, Nancy, from there; but come
in, sir; come in, it's cold out here, and we must
have a blazing hearth and a comfortable chat
over this.   And as for the secret, why it's as
safe as ever it can be anywheres.   Guess as
guess can, none shall be the wiser for I.

Come in, sir. Holloa there, Bobbie, some wood on the fire. Nancy—Nancy—why here be—"

"Hold!" said Edgar, "is that how you keep secrets?"

"Why, Nancy lived wi'un," exclaimed Hopkins, "it was from the baronet's as I married her, didn't I? She wur but a poor skinny thing then, in spite o' your granfa—; I mean the gentleman's cupboard; but now look what she be, there ain't a plumper dame in—"

"What be talking about, Chars?" asked the full faced, portly dame, who entered at this moment, wiping her fat arms with her apron. "What be talking about, Chars? thee'st had the morning glass, I'm thinking; and it be early too for thic!"

"I say, didn't thee come from Zomzetshire, Nancy?" said Hopkins.

"And what then, Chars? What has thic to do wi' thee, now, or the young gentleman? thee know'st where I be come from without my tellin' thee."

"And didn't thee live wi' old Sir George Morton?"

"Sure enough, Chars," answered Nancy, unable as yet to comprehend the drift of the examination. "And what then?'"

"And didn't I marry thee like a good feller, Nancy?"

"What nonsense thee do talk, Chars; sure enough did thee; but what then?"

"Thee wast but a skinny lass when I married thee, and now thee bee'st as fat—"

"Get out with thee, Chars, thee'st had the morning cup, I tell thee."

"Look here," said Hopkins, in a half whisper, drawing his bulky spouse aside, and in front of Edgar, "this gentleman be Sir George's grandchild."

"Lor, Chars," exclaimed Nancy, "what bee'st thee talkin' about, thic fashion."

"It's true, I tell thee, I swear it;" and Charles's hand thumped the table like a sledge hammer.

"The Lord bless thee, sir; who ha' thought it,

but I see the gentleman's got master's eyes, and the very forehead of my lady, and my lady's smile, and my lady's nose—why, so it be, Chars;" and Mrs. Hopkins made a very obeisant, but by no means graceful, curtsey.

Edgar began to think that a little further examination of his features and person would make him " my lady " herself; but Mrs. Hopkins was too overjoyed to proceed with her scrutiny, since, with true feminine curiosity, she was anxious to learn the intentions of her guest; as to whether he had come to take possession of Heathmoor, and so on; all which questions Edgar answered without hesitation, but with some little precaution, since his belief in his host's capacity for keeping secrets was somewhat shaken by recent experience.

" Go thee, Nancy, and put on thy best gown, for thee must not sit down with us, thic figure," said Hopkins.

But Nancy, fearing lest some part of the story should escape her if she left the room, wrapped

her apron around her naked elbows and stood
between her husband and her guest, in front of
the fire, which, under the superintendence of a
lean country lad, who knew as much of the
English language as he did of manners, stood
fanning the struggling flame with his tattered
cap.

"Now thee can go, Robert," said Hopkins,
" and if thy brains 'll brighten as fast as thic fire
here, thee'll soon want a better cap to cover 'em
wi', and it 'll be no thanks to thy fanning; did'st
go to church yesterday, Bobbie ?"

" Yees, sir," said the boy.

" And where were thic text ?"

" Text, sir," said the boy, scratching his head,
the hair of which protruded through his cap. " It
be too long agoo, sir—I forgets."

" Did'st have dinner yesterday, Robert?" asked
his master.

" Yees, sir, sure, did ur."

" What did'st have ?"

" Pork and greens and taters, sir."

" I thought thee'd know thic," said Hopkins.

" But 'tain't allays same text, sir; paarson wobbles about so there's no cotchin' him in one plaace."

" Dost mean to say, thee scamp, that thee always has pork and greens for dinner ?"

" Noo, sir."

" Dost have belly full ?"

" Yees, sir."

" Hast got a good master ?"

" Yees, sir."

" Wast playing pitch and toss on tombstone, I warrant thee, instead o' praying."

Bob looked awfully thunderstricken, as he declared that he was in church during the whole service.

" Dost like playin' or prayin' best, Bobbie ?"

" Prayin' sure, sir," answered Bob, with a grin.

" Thee bee'st a liar," said Hopkins, " why thic grin o' thine shines down thic throat and shows the lie—thee hypocrite. Dost know who made thee, Robert ?"

"They says Tom the blacksmith," answered Robert.

"There's a pretty fellow for a parson," said Hopkins. "We talk, sir, of makin a parson of this feller."

"Here, my man," said Edgar, "here is something to buy a Bible with."

"Thank'ee, sir—thank'ee, sir," said Robert, pulling the hair which hung over his forehead.

"Wilt buy a Bible, Bobby?" asked Hopkins.

"Yees, sir, sure, will 'ur," said the boy.

"Thee confounded rogue; it wur only last night thee wur up to thy pranks in thic larder—a pretty Bible thee'll buy, I'll warrant thee. Hast been up to Heathmoor lately?"

"No, sir, not since dame Wilmerton went away."

"And how's that, Bobby?"

"Nobody dare goo now, sir; the keeper there's got orders to turn 'em all away."

"Who did'st like best, Bobbie, the old housekeeper or the last."

" The last one by odds, sir; she wur a good 'un, so was miss—"

" Now go and buy thic Bible, and learn un by heart mind," said Hopkins; and the boy, grinning almost from ear to ear, left the apartment.

"A cunning dog," said Hopkins, " he's so artful, sir, that I bleeve sometimes he really be the devil."

" He would do," said Edgar, " if some pains were bestowed upon him, but he wants a deal of pruning."

" He wants diggin' up and fresh plantin'," said Hopkins, " but that's master parson's business, not mine. Now, Nancy," he added, as he saw her return in her fancy dress, which had been put on during the time of the conversation with Robert ; " Now, Nancy, we must be silent about this gentleman, for no one knows what's coming on't."

" Sure enough, Chars; but lor, lor, how like my lady! it do seem that I see my lady this very minute."

" Will thee hold thic tongue, Nancy ?"

" Now, Mr. Hopkins," said Edgar, "since I have so far made you my confidant, will you tell me anything you know respecting the young woman that was lately at Heathmoor ?"

Mrs. Hopkins and her husband commenced replying at the same moment, but a sharp rebuke from the jolly landlord quickly put to silence for the time being his loquacions better half—the other half proceeded thus—

"Thee knows, sir, that some three year ago, Mrs. Wilmington and her daughter comed here, that be to Heathmoor, and soon after a new keeper, Jack Thornbury, as surly a brute as ever beat cover. For a long time the tale went as to the why and the wherefore of these new servants, the more specially as the place were already what we'd 'a called overstocked; but soon after it wur told here, in this werry room, how the son of Squire Hindly, which wur thee, sir—excuse my freedom—had 'fended thic father and gone to Lonnon, where thee wur said to be living like the prod'gal son, running into a pig trough with thee fortune. Then comed tales about how thee had tooked away this poor gal from thic, and hurt the gal's character, which thee know, sir, can't be mended in this world."

"By Heaven!" exclaimed Edgar, "the blackguard that could promulgate such a falsehood—but proceed, sir—proceed."

"How like my lady he do look, surely, when my lady were piqued," said Mrs. Hopkins.

"Hold thic tongue, Nancy, let's out wi' it, for it must all be told now. Well, sir, they do say that thee desartin' the poor lady—for she ware as ladylike as a duchess—drove her to drinkin'."

"Lor, Chars, 'twere better say no more."

"But I *will* say it, sir—every word shall come out; whether she drinked hard or not, sir, I don't know; but I never shall bleeve it, if I lives a thousand year, and wur told it every day. But she wur one day found unsensible in her private room; the doctor wur sent for, and the tale soon spread that it wur as I telled thee."

"But when was this, my friend soon after her arrival at Heathmoor?"

"Just before her went away, for the talk so runned that her never went out after till the news of her bad habits reached the Squire's ears, and he sent her off."

"Go on," said Edgar, whose emotion had somewhat checked the innkeeper, and caused him to fortify his spirits by a copious draught of ale.

"It seems," continued the landlord, "that in spite of her love affair with thee, thic Jack Thornbury made up to her; and they do say as how the Squire offered five hundred pounds to marry her."

"It were a thousand pound, Chars," interrupted Mrs. Hopkins.

"Peace! I tell thee, Nancy; if I can't tell my own story, I don't know how the devil thee can tell it for I. It might ha' been a thousand, sir, I won't say; but the gal wouldn't have him at no price, although I will say she were foolish to walk wi' 'un."

" Did she walk with him ?" asked Edgar.

" Hold your tongue, Chars !" said Mrs. Hopkins.

" Her wur wi' 'un, round by thic other side o' thic pond one night—the very night, I bleeve, before her left—there, where thee sees thic clump of firs on th' other side of thic common."

" But how do you know this ?" asked Edgar.

" From that Bobbie o' ours, who were out laying eel-lines thereabouts wi thic boat; but stop, sir, thee shall hear the tale first hands. Bobbie! Bobbie!" he shouted, till the whole house resounded.

" Stay !" said Edgar, " he's too shrewd a lad to be called expressly for the purpose of asking such a question."

" I'll manage un all right, sir; be easy. Here, Bobbie, some more firing, that's a good lad. Know'd what I wanted, didn't thee, Bobbie ?"

" Yees, sir," squeaked Bobbie. Bobbie's voice was " breaking."

Another faggot was heaped upon the embers,

and truckled up together by the accomplished stoker, whose principal business seemed to be to prepare faggots for that purpose.

" Many eels hast caught this morning, Bobbie ?" asked Hopkins.

" None, sir, only a lampin," replied the youth, screwing his eyes into the oddest possible shape.

" None ! thee beest a purty fisherman."

" Wants some thunder, sir, to make un bite," said Robert.

" That's more than thee dost ; I'll go to hell if thee doesn't bite well without thunder. Be dinner ready ?"

" Dunnow, sir."

" Beest thee ready ?"

" Yees, sir."

" I be hanged if thee were a fish, if a bait o' fat pork wouldn't any time haul thee out o' water. This be the rascal, sir, that watches young men and women when they court, beant thee Bob ?"

Bob hardly knew how to reply with words, so he confessed the fact by a very broad grin, and a very cunning leer at the gentleman.

" Didn't thee catch 'em purty one night, Bobbie, eh ?"

" Yees, sir."

" What wur 'em doing, Bob ?"

" Thornbury got un's arm round the young
ooman's throat."

" And what then ?"

" She screamed out when she seed I," said
Bobbie.

" And what then ?"

" She 'most tumbled in thic water."

" And if her had tumbled in," said Mrs. Hopkins, " woulds't thee pulled her out ?"

" Yees," said Robert.

" A purty fellow to pull her out," said the
husband ; " what did un do then ?"

" He let goo when he seed I," answered Bob.

" Did he kiss her, Bob ?   I'll warrant ur did."

" Dunnow, sir.   I eeard her 'oller, and then he
went off, and she run'd round t'other way."

Edgar felt more deeply than words could express, and appeared from that moment to take an

D 2

interest in the uncouth boy. In spite of his feelings, and probably the better to conceal them, he enquired if the youth had ever been to school.

Bob, to whom this question was addressed, brushed the hair aside from his forehead, drew his cuff across his nose, and pronounced a very audible, but at the same time very squeaky, " Yees, sir."

The landlord laughed to himself, and then at Bobbie, as he asked—

" Where be thy learnin' then? A purty feller thee beest to go to school; why, thee doen't know which letter thic alphbet begins with, I'll warrant thee; where didst go to school then?"

" Sunday-school, sir, up at parish," answered Bobbie.

" And who taught thee there."

" Miss Wilmerton, while she bided hereabouts," said the youth.

" A purty fellow," rejoined Hopkins; " and now thee tellst tales of her, does thee? What didst learn then? not to take off cap when gentleman speaks to thee, I'll warrant. And now harkee, I'll cut of thic hair that sticks up through un like rushes on a marsh, if thee can't keep it in better fashion."

Bob took the hint, pulled off his remnant of cap, and stroked his shaggy head two or three times by way of inducing it to lie down; but in spite of his efforts, it still stood up.

"Thee beest a purty feller to go to school; and what didst learn, Bible?"

"Yees, sir," said Bob.

"And what there? dost know who made thee?"

Robert grinned till the question was repeated, when he answered—

"Gord, sir."

"And who were the first man?"

"Hadn't got so fur as that, sir."

Hopkins laughed.

"Thee be a purty fellow for a parson—there, that'll do; hast fed the pigs?"

"No, sir, were guine to."

"Well, go to it," said Hopkins, whereupon

Robert slunk from the apartment. He was no sooner gone than the landlord, pulling the faggot together with the hooked iron which was kept for that purpose, addressed himself to Edgar.

"Thee sees, sir, it be true; the young woman was with thic fellow Thornbury, as th' lad said."

"Of that I have not the least doubt," replied Edgar; "but my suspicions are more than ever confirmed, and if anything were wanting to establish the innocence of the girl's character, the circumstances you have alluded to would be sufficient. Who was the doctor that attended her at the time?"

"Doctor Jeffery," said Hopkins, "they calls un; but I have no bleef in un."

"Nor I, Chars," said Mrs. Hopkins; "he be more like to kill nor cure, any day. Dost remember how he poisoned poor old Gumbley?"

"Poisoned!" exclaimed Edgar.

"Yes," said Hopkins, "he give Gumbley the wrong physic; there, it be all done, and we needn't bring up thic."

"And where is this villain Thornbury now?" asked Edgar.

"Well, 'tis said that he seed strange sights about the old 'ouse," said the landlord; "and they soon had it that the house were haunted, though I do bleeve there be something in that, mind."

Edgar smiled.

"There be strange noises," said Mrs. Hopkins, "at night."

"Especially, I suppose," said Edgar, "when it's rather stormy and the shutters rattle; but what has become of Mrs. Wilmington and her daughter? Have you no idea as to where they live, or what they are doing?"

"Not a bit," said Mrs. Hopkins; "my heart do feel for 'em, sure. They bided here one night, and I wish they'd stayed longer; but the poor girl seemed downright heartbroked. I'm afraid she be dead."

"Why do you think so?" asked Edward.

"She were so pale and delicate-like, poor

thing; I seem to think it wur better to took the money."

" Hold thic tongue !" said Hopkins, " she were too good for thic feller, and all the gold in the Inges wouldn't ha' made he better. Tut upon marryin' up to such as he, thee took care to marry a good feller when thee got switched ; an I dunnow to this day whether thee married I for money or goodness. Thee were but a poor skinny thing when I took thee, and now look what thee beest."

" Lor, Chars, how thee do talk," said Nancy. " He worritted I, sir, to that degree, that I were forced to marry up to un to get rid of un."

" Well," said Edgar, " I shall proceed to the Hall, maybe I shall hear something further of this Thornbury. You will be good enough to keep a bed for me this evening ; but let the matter of my visit be kept quiet. And now for my reckoning—no, Hopkins, keep the change, don't want a bill, will that satisfy you ?"

" I will take no such payment," said Hopkins;

" when gentlemen come to my house, they sha'n't be robbed thic fashion. Nancy, the gentleman's bill."

" But I insist," said Edgar, " and many thanks for your kindness."

" I shall let the company drink your health then this blessed night," said the landlord, " in the best wine I got in th' cellar."

" Not a word of me, I pray," said Edgar.

" But you be going to Heathmoor," answered Hopkins, " and I warrant thee there beant a child at Sunday school but 'll talk on't."

" Not till after my departure at all events," said Edgar ; " Till then keep quiet."

Thus saying, Edgar took leave of the good natured host and hostess ; and, after requesting them to send on his portmanteau in case he should not return by a certain hour, left the inn, and proceeded in the direction of Heathmoor.

CHAPTER IV.

" PARCHMENT, TAPE, AND CO."

As before intimated the mansion of Heathmoor
was situated in a wild and romantic part of the
country. It had probably been built in the early
part of the reign of Edward the Third, and con-
sisted chiefly of a large oblong building, pre-
tending somewhat to the Gothic order, but
constructed without any further attempt at design
than was usual at the rude period of its erection;
perhaps the later additions that had been made,
in the shape of two projecting wings, had given

a more decided character to the edifice than its
first architects attempted, more especially as the
windows, originally square, had been altered to
the sharp, angular Gothic which, if rendering it
more sombre, at the same time gave it a more
picturesque appearance. Two octagonal towers
flanked each wing, while the angle formed by the
projection of the newer buildings was relieved by
three sided towers, ornamented at each storey
with layers of stone, in which narrow windows in the shape of slits or fissures broke
the monotonous aspect of the sombre brickwork.
Each tower was surmounted by a castellated
parapet, finishing at the angles in a turret that
still preserved some of its original carving,
although time had obliterated whatever device it
once bore. The principal door was composed of
two thick oaken leaves studded with massive
iron; while a heavy twisted ring depended from
the centre. The grounds were extensive, and
although overgrown with brambles and weeds,
still preserved the outline of their gravel drives

and paths, showing that at one time its owner had
spared neither expense nor skill in rendering
them beautiful. The fish-ponds were coated with
a green mantle of weeds, and the untrained shrubs
and bushes completely obscured their once graceful margin. It was a grand ruin that presented
itself to the eye of Edgar as he pushed open the
dilapidated postern gate in the crumbling wall
which enclosed the grounds. Branches, unpruned
and untrained, were dangling in heavy festoons
from the high garden wall on the right, while a
great deal of the rustic fence to the left, which
had once divided the lawn from the park beyond,
lay strewn by the wind in all directions; some
portions, however, were still leaning against the
ancient oaks and other trees, which formed a
pleasing and picturesque avenue as far as the eye
could reach. In some places whole panels were
embedded in the luxuriant grass which had overgrown it, so little trouble had the occupants of
this ruined mansion taken to preserve it from
utter desolation.

Edgar proceeded to the garden in the hope of meeting some one or other of the lazy guardians of this wilderness before entering the mansion, where he had reason to anticipate that his reception would be far from agreeable, especially as he expected to encounter the little man with the green spectacles who had somewhat too freely disclosed his business on the previous night. A patch or two of cabbages and other vegetables was all that indicated the probability of human existence in this uncultivated scene.

Edgar looked around him with that feeling of melancholy which always seems, more or less, to possess one when contemplating scenes which speak of better days. The phantom of the past was everywhere around him, and the very sigh of the wind seemed like an echo of bygone times.

" This then," thought he, " is mine, the inheritance to which I have succeeded—but how? Heaven knows, my very prosperity is adversity; my fortune, ruin; my father is my worst enemy; my friends have guided me to the precincts of a jail; my love has cursed me and my own heart betrayed me; the citadel has yielded to the treachery of its defender, while even the proud man that once called me son, failed to conquer. All this for her; a penniless, but beautiful girl! Love, love, thou hast played the devil with me; angel like in thy form, thou camest to me with ruin under thy wing. But I *will* have her, though ten times discarded. She is virtuous in spite of all. Calumny, slander, ay, the devil himself cannot invent a tale that can gain credence with me."

His thoughts were interrupted by a man who strolled lazily into the garden with a spade on his shoulder, and a short pipe in his mouth. He was somewhat advanced in years, though of a ruddy, healthy countenance, and, to all appearance, by no means a stranger to good living. As he approached Edgar he raised his hand to his cap, and, in a voice, which was more authoritative than respectful, demanded his business.

"My business is not with you, my friend," replied Hindly.

"Then, sir, you has no business here," rejoined the gardener, for such was his profession.

Edgar smiled. " Do you know, my friend, to whom you speak?" he demanded.

The old man knocked out the ashes of his pipe on the handle of his spade as he replied—

" It matters leetle, sir, who I speak to, so as I knows you ain't no right here."

" And who has, pray?" asked Edgar.

" Oh! that's it," said the old man, " there's bin a good many comed here claiming the place, like, but Jack Wilson's master here."

" And who's Jack Wilson, my friend?"

" I be," said the old man.

" And the place is yours, is it?"

" They can't turn I out, anyhow," answered the gardener.

" I suppose," said Edgar, " some one pays your wages?"

" For that 'ere matter," answered Wilson, " it's my binness, not yourn; there's the geat, sir, and I should 'vise yer—"

"Stay," said Edgar, "before you proceed further, let me order you to take the path you are suggesting to me; your services are no longer required here."

Wilson laughed; and at that moment another appeared on the scene, in the person of the keeper, Thornbury.

"What dy'e think," said Wilson, "there's another o' them Lunneners;" and sticking the spade into the ground he planted his foot upon the shoulder of it, and stood grinning, first at Edgar, and then at Thornbury, who advanced towards them with a gun under his arm, followed by a shaggy and savage dog of the mastiff species, which, the moment it saw the stranger, commenced a fierce and ominous growl. Thornbury, however, restrained it from rushing upon Edgar, by shouting to it in a voice scarcely less savage than that of the dog itself.

"Thornbury!" said Edgar.

The keeper bowed slightly, or rather, nodded; but his countenance seemed to indicate strong and irrepressible emotion, as though shame and vulgar pride were equally influencing him.

"What do you, here, Thornbury?" asked Edgar; "and who is this that dares to insult me on my own premises?"

"For what I does here," answered Thornbury, "you might 'ave saved yourself the journey, for the Squire could ha' answered the question."

Edgar felt the insolence of the remark, and turned away in contempt, towards the gate which led to the house, disdaining to hold further conference with these impudent menials.

"Beg pardon, sir," said Thornbury, "but yer mor'nt goo in."

"What!" exclaimed Edgar, in a tone of anger.

"Yer mor'nt goo in, sir; such is my orders," replied Thornbury.

"Who dares oppose me?" asked Edgar, with a look of disdain.

"I've got orders, sir."

"From whom?"

"The Squire."

"Look," said Edgar, "the Squire himself, were he here, would try to prevent me at his peril. Say no more; and follow me, if you dare."

There was an air of boldness and determination in the countenance of Edgar that for awhile made even Thornbury irresolute; he paused, and allowing Edgar to proceed, followed him at a respectful distance. Even the peremptory commands of his employer seemed empty before the stern and determined demeanour of his son; and Thornbury felt that it would be dangerous to interfere. Edgar hastily quitted the garden, and, although his temper was usually calm, and scarcely ever passionate, for once it seemed to gain the mastery of his judgment, for, lifting the latch of the kitchen door, and finding it resisted his attempts to open it, he dashed his foot against the heavy oaken panel, and instantly it gave way; the staple, already loosened in the partially rotten post, flew into the chamber, and fell with a ringing sound upon the stone pavement. · A shriek from an elderly female echoed

through the ancient house, and was quickly succeeded by another in response. Edgar, however,
disregarding ceremony, pushed his way into the
hall, whither dame Elderly, the housekeeper, had
retreated.

" What—who—pray, sir, spare me—spare us,"
exclaimed two females at the same instant.

" Spare you; what do you mean?" asked
Edgar. "Do you know me?"

" Lor, sir—sir," said Elderly, affecting an appearance of great alarm, " I thought—I thought
—I did think—O, lor—"

" Thought what, my good woman?"

" It was thieves, sir; you see we be so lonely
down here."

" My name is Hindly," said Edgar, without
further ceremony.

" Yes, sir; yes, sir," said the housekeeper.

At this moment the little gentleman with the
green spectacles shuffled into the hall; and, as he
turned up his face towards Edgar, the flash of his
little eyes was clearly discernible through the

glasses. His hands were involuntarily uplifted, and his whole appearance indicated surprise and terror, as though he instantly recalled his conversation of the preceding evening.

By this time Edgar had become calmer; and, surveying the grotesque little gentleman for some moments, as though startled with the sudden apparition of his former companion, he advanced a step or two towards him, and said—

" My name is Hindly, sir; may I request the favour of yours ?"

" Sir, at your service.   Mr. Parchment, sir, of the firm of Parchment, Tape, and Co., New Inn."

" Indeed !" said Edgar.   " If I mistake not, I had the honour of being in your company last evening."

" Really, sir," said Parchment, as if endeavouring to recollect the circumstance.   " You see, sir, travellers, you know, meet with many strangers ; and — why, yes, I think I *do* recollect your face."

" I thought lawyers were usually noted for keen observation and retentive memories," said Edgar. " You may remember, perhaps, that you were speaking of one, Edgar Hindly, at the ' Talbot."

" You see, sir, it is our business to learn all we can. And—yes, let me think—yes, I certainly *did* converse with those that I thought were very likely to know about this unfortunate business."

" What unfortunate business ?" asked Edgar.

" Well, sir," said Parchment, " if you—perhaps you will accompany me to my room ; — Mrs. Elder—hem—"

" Elder*ly*, if you please, sir," said the housekeeper.

" Ly, ly ; I beg pardon, Mrs. Elderly ; yes, to be sure—*ly*—I remember. Some candles, if you please ; and Mr. Hindly will take some refreshment."

" Not of your bounty, sir," answered Edgar, " in my own house, if you please. You will allow

me to give orders here, while you will be good
enough to explain the nature of your business."

"Will you take a seat, sir?" said Parchment.

"Stay," said Edgar, "and understand me, Mr.
Parchment. I think it the height of impudence
in you to take these unpardonable liberties, and
to assume this counterfeit air of authority."

"Counterfeit!" exclaimed Parchment, in a
tone of anger. "The firm of Parchment, Tape,
and Co., sir, is one of the most respectable in the
metropolis; and 1 will not permit you, sir, or
anyone else, with impunity, sir, to stigmatize it
as a counterfeit. Have at you, sir, with an action
on the case."

Edgar, in spite of his feelings, could scarcely
repress a smile, although it was one of bitter contempt and disdain.

"I will tell you what it is," he answered, "I
shall take the liberty of putting you out of these
doors, unless you desist from insulting me."

"Mrs. Elderly, is—is the constable here?"

asked Parchment; "my life, I see, is imperilled in this business."

"He *were* 'ere," said the trembling woman; "but, oh! dear, sir, surely you and the young master can settle without a bother. Mr. Hindly, sir, I'm sure, I'm ready to give up to you, sir— the place ain't *mine*."

"Thank you," said Edgar; "I presume it's yours then, Mr. Parchment?"

"Well, not exactly," said the legal gentleman; "that will do, Mrs. Elderly."

And the good lady made her exit, while Mr. Parchment proceeded.

"You see, sir, the estate belonged to Mrs. Hindly; and, your father wanting a little money, obtained her consent to a mortgage. However, that has nothing to do with the case, which it is at present my duty, under your father's instructions, to lay before you. You see, sir, whatever estates of freehold a wife *has*, the husband is entitled to what is called the *curtesy*, that is, sir, by the *curtesy of England*, he is entitled to them for his *life,* under certain circumstances, issue that could *inherit,* and so on ; hem !"

"And that little piece of legal phraseology, you presume upon," said Edgar, "to postpone my claim, do you ?"

"The law *gives* it to him," said Parchment, "the *law,* sir ; and really, sir, I should advise you, under existing circumstances—pardon me, sir, I speak as a *friend*—to submit quietly."

"Comfortable advice, truly," said Edgar ; "you advise me to be just so big a fool as will advance your own interest, do you, Mr. Parchment ?"

"It will be to *your* interest, sir, not *mine*—not mine, sir," said the lawyer.

"Well," said Edgar, "we can reduce this matter to a small compass ; let Mrs. Elderly and the rest of the household enter, if you please."

Mr. Parchment, who began to think from Edgar's manner that he contemplated violence, shuffled a little in his seat ; and, as the two house-keepers entered in obedience to the summons,

Mr. Parchment again enquired for the constable, " merely," he said, " as a *witness*."

The constable, who had in the meantime been sent for, entered ; a short, thick-set, chubby shoe-maker, who had on his leathern-apron, under a huge drab coat.

" Constable," said Edgar, " you will be good enough to listen attentively to what is about to take place between this gentleman and myself."

The constable wiped his mouth with his coat-sleeve, and bowed.

" Now, Mr. Parchment," continued Edgar, "I am here to take possession of my estate ; you are here, you say, to prevent me."

" Pardon me, sir," said Parchment, " but the curtesy—"

" D—— the curtesy !" said Edgar.

" Ay," said Parchment, a little ruffled ; " it may be a d—— inconvenience to heirs-at-law, but it's not to be blotted out of the *custom* of England by a curse."

The constable looked as though he understood

very little of what they were saying, except that they were swearing a good deal.

" You see, sir," continued Parchment, " your father is *entitled* while he *lives*."

" And you mean to say that you are here to prevent my taking possession. Is that it, Mr. Parchment?"

" To explain the nature of the circumstances, sir, I am here; hem! that is all, sir."

" Am I to have possession ?"

" Your father's instructions, sir—"

" Answer my question, Mr. Parchment. Am I to have possession ?"

" N—n—no, sir; hem! no, sir—not *quite* that."

" Enough !" answered Edgar; " at whose command am I ejected ?"

" Not *ejected*, sir; you see ejectment—is, legally—the *putting out* of possession. You, sir, are not *in* possession—not in, sir."

" Cut your legal jargon, Mr. Parchment, and tell me who claims, and who holds against me."

" Your father, sir."

" Very well. I suppose you will have no objection to my taking possession of certain papers and trinkets which belonged to my mother, and which are in a certain cabinet here ?"

" My orders, sir, are express and implicit," replied Parchment; " and that cabinet, in particular, is to be guarded against all intrusion. Your father holds it sacred, and is in great concern that he cannot find the key of it. Your late mother, poor dear lady, had kept it, it seems, in a little secret drawer of her bureau until the day before her death ; but by whom it has been taken therefrom he cannot say; but, I must confess, sir, that his suspicions are confirmed by what you have now stated—for the secret drawer showed tokens of having been opened with some violence."

" What do you mean, sir ?" asked Edgar, angrily.

" I don't insinuate anything, sir," replied Parchment, " I merely tell you what your father's suspicions were; it's for you, sir, to judge whether they are right or wrong, and to put upon them a construction according to your own knowledge. Plainly, sir, he suspected you of having taken it; hem!"

"God help me!" exclaimed Edgar, "such a father makes me hate the very name I bear. My mother gave me, with her own hand, the key of that cabinet; and, mark me, Parchment, what's there is mine, and I will have it."

"Very sorry," said Parchment, "for the unfortunate position in which I am placed; but threats, sir—threats cannot avail you; take my advice and wait the issue patiently; in these matters, sir, it's always best to be patient."

"The issue," said Edgar, "will not be long postponed. Heaven must do justice. My fathe has robbed me! robbed me!"

And the unhappy young man rose from his seat and turned towards the door, overcome with excitement.

Mrs. Elderly, in spite of her fears lest she

should lose the excellent situation of mistress of Heathmoor, could not conceal her emotion as Edgar turned from the lawyer, who had met him armed with a father's cruel authority. To deprive him of his estate was bad enough, she thought—albeit, a very good thing so far as she was concerned; but to prevent him from taking the last gifts of his dying mother, was like mocking her in her grave, and hooting her to the gate of heaven. Mrs. Elderly held her apron to her eyes and cried; then, hastening after Edgar, she took his hand and begged him to take some refreshment.

"Thank you for your kindness, Mrs. Elderly," said he; "but if I have no right here, I will not keep my foot on it longer than I can help. If this house is my father's you are offering me his food; and, by Heaven, I have eaten my last morsel from his table. He who deprives me of my birthright would deprive me of my soul if he could."

Thus saying, Edgar left the Hall, and passing

down the avenue, made his exit by the postern, and proceeded by the same way that he had come, towards the "Talbot," where a heartier welcome awaited him than he had received at Heath-moor.

CHAPTER V.

THE PARISH CONSTABLE.

HOPKINS and his bulky wife entertained the heir of Heathmoor in their private room—a token of special favour, which was duly appreciated, the more so as Edgar's position was now one of peculiar discomfort and hardship. No one so truly appreciates friendship and sympathy as he upon whom the world has turned its darker side; and none can understand the feelings of the unfortunate youth at that moment except those who have experienced the world's bitter frown. With a sad heart, he took his seat by the parlour fire. Memory hovered over the past, and the dim visions of former days flitted through his mind.

Hopkins could not but observe the air of abstraction which seemed to involve his guest, and his question of "How didst get on up at House, sir?" was repeated before Edgar recollected where he was.

"It's ill with me, my good friend; ill—very ill—they have robbed me of all."

"Hem!" said Hopkins, "thee don't say so, sir. Thic man with the green spectacles, I s'pose?"

"Yes," said Edgar, "he's my father's lawyer, it seems, and claims all; so long as he lives, I am houseless. He has completed his injustice at last, and crowned it all by robbing my mother in her grave, and depriving me of even my birthright."

Edgar then narrated the whole of the circumstances, which are already in the knowledge of the reader.

" Never thee mind," said Mrs. Hopkins, as she prepared the tea; "thee'll be righted yet, I feel't, and thic Thornbury 'll come to no good."

"Hold thic tongue, Nancy," said Hopkins; "it's not for thee to spake 't; gie him a rope, and he'll use it in the best fashion, I'll warrant thee; he wur born wi' a broken neck."

"Sure enough was ur born wi' a broken neck, Chars," repeated the landlady; "and gardener Wilson were ever an old thief, mark me."

"Hush! I tell thee," said Hopkins; "if thee gettst on thic fashion, the'll hang 'alf the village, and then the 'Talbot' 'll have to close its shutters in mourning for its customers."

"They're all a bad lot down hereabouts, Mr. Hindly, ready to cut a throat for a penny or a drink o' beer; sure enough they're the worst lot I ever 'eerd of, and I know it's false about poor Lizzy Wilmington drinking and getting wi' ch—"

"Tut! tut!" interposed Hopkins, half good-humouredly, yet manifesting some concern lest his wife's melodious tongue, which retained its

E 5

Somersetshire twang, should get her into difficulties.

"What do you refer to?" asked Edgar.

"I told thee how 'tud be," said Hopkins;
"thee'dst better had thy tongue out instead o'
thic tooth t'other day, for I mind it when thic tooth
ached well, there wur more peace for I than there
been ever since, though it wur a devil to see thee
mewed up in thic arm chair, and swaying to and
fro like a cobbler mendin' shoes, wi' face swelled
up like a sweed turmut."

"You need fear nothing from what I shall
divulge," said Edgar, anxious to glean any
further information respecting the lost girl.

"Well," said Hopkins, drawing towards him
and whispering in his ear, although with a voice
almost loud enough to be heard in the public
room; "there wur a child found buried in
Heathmoor Garden, newly born; but there I
have a mind to say it wur no more hers than it
wor mine."

The effect of this communication on Edgar was

far from that which Mr. Hopkins had anticipated ;
he sipped his port negus and cast a meditative
glance at the huge log which was sending up its
lively flames into the chimney.   After a pause of
a few moments he enquired where it was and
what proceedings were taken in the matter, these
questions simply eliciting the information that
the course of law had been taken, that the really
guilty parties had escaped suspicion, and that the
enquiry had been so conducted as to lead to the
defamation of the character of the innocent.

"I shall leave you this evening," said Edgar,
"for I must go at once to London."

"Nay," interrupted Hopkins, "thee'dst better
bide wi us to-night, may be something 'll turn
up, and it's no night for travelling a journey like
thic. I'd a mind to ask thee to stay a week, sir ;
my house shall be at your service for the sake of
the good old master, Sir George.   I should
respeck the hobnail of his shootin' boot if I could
find un.   I'm grieved, sir—grieved that his

grandson should be treated thic fashion by his father; but may be he's a bit trying thee, and—who knows—I wouldn't be hasty, for thic green-eyed lawyer might do thee service, and if he's what I took un for last night we shall pick the brains of un in another night. Thee mind, sir, the fireside in a public wi' lively company, and grog, such as Nancy brews, bean't the worst place in the world for looking into a man's sky-light; many a secret had never been out if thic grog hadn't been in, and boozing comrades be all bosom friends, and secrets out like water from one pond to another, an' the best talker's the worst winner."

" I think *thee* be no winner then, Chars, for thee talkst fast enough."

" A gallopping horse and a scolding woman; what have I told thee these be like, Nancy."

" Thee be always at thy nonsense, Chars."

" Now get thee some wine, gal ; lor, thee wur but a skinny thing when—"

" Hold thic nonsense, Chars," interrupted Mrs. Hopkins, as she rose to get the wine. " Here be thic gardener."

Hopkins rose as a knock at the bar counter summoned him to that department, anxious to hear Wilson's account of the day's proceedings. However, there was little to be gleaned from him except that the gentleman, Mr. Parchment, was going to give them a treat in honour of the squire, and by way of acknowledgment for the care and attention they had bestowed upon the estate of Heathmoor; but, doubtless, with the object of repaying them for the zeal they had displayed in calumniating the Wilmington party, and sending them so promptly about their business, whatever and wherever that business might be.

In spite of the host's cordial invitation to remain another night, Edgar resolved upon setting out on his dreary and hopeless journey, feeling that there was little to be got by way of information respecting her for whose welfare he was more anxious than his own, and sick at heart with the slanderous reports which every tongue seemed to bring.

But the elder wine was smoking upon the hearth, and the praises of Hopkins must be exhausted before he could be allowed to depart, and, in truth, with Edgar it was almost a matter of indifference what course he took or whither he went; probably a sense of shame urged upon him an immediate departure from the " Talbot," rather than expose himself to the village gaze after so signal a defeat as he had sustained. And yet Edgar seldom heeded the opinion of the vulgar crowd, whose applause is equally as worthy of contempt as is its censure.

As the evening wore on and the time for the starting of the mail approached, Edgar prepared for his departure. Hopkins swore a superb oath that he would not take another penny by way of recompense, and Mrs. Hopkins was equally vehement, although not so violent in her protestations.

" It be not often, sir," said the former, " that
we 'ave to take care customers don't pay twice;
but the next time my house is honoured wi'
thy company I'll take care thee doesn't pay
once, so good luck to thee, sir—Sir Edgar, I'll
call thee Sir Edgar—and, Nancy, mind I'll chop
thy legs off if thee ever takes a penny of un."

"Thee sha'nt chop my legs off, Chars, on no
such score," said Nancy.

" If you hear anything," said Edgar, " do not
fail to let me know; this address will find me."

" Right," answered the good-natured host;
" I'll have the news as sure as the *Times* paper.
There's little done hereabouts but gets to the
parlour of the 'Talbot'—good or bad it comes here;
but I'd have thee stay to-night, sir. There's a
good lot in the room now, and the mail might
bring noos—who knows?—and there it be.
Now where be thic Bobbie, Nancy? snoring, I'll
warrant thee, by kitchen fire."

As he spoke the coach drew up, and after a few
minutes occupied in changing horses and supply-

ing the ordinary refreshments to coachman, guard, and passengers, Edgar was once more on his way to London.

The following evening was one of momentous importance at the "Talbot," for all day rumours had been afloat of a daring burglary that had been committed at Heathmoor; at first the startling intelligence was circulated that every one of the inmates of the mansion had been murdered. The news, however, as the day wore on, became somewhat modified, and at last it was ascertained that only the dog had been murdered, although Thornbury had received a severe flagellation at the hands of the burglars, after having been tied to the bedpost. There was much travelling to and fro towards Heathmoor, and a great deal of measuring tracks, apertures, and broken casements by that sharp and well trained official, the parish constable. Having written down the exact measurement of the footprints in their length and breadth, and resorted to the scientific dodge of covering them carefully over with drain tiles

so that there should be no possibility of their
being effaced, the powerful functionary of the law
was at length accidentally furnished with a far
more substantial clue to the ruffians, for in a
little recess by the postern gate he discovered the
shoes that exactly fitted the tracks. This was
important, that was, if the footprints were. Toby
Quarterman carefully wrapped up the shoes in a
blue and white handkerchief, and, as the language
of the constabulary hath it, "took charge of
them." Having made the necessary survey he
came to the conclusion that the robbery had not
been committed by any one *in* the house, since
the little lawyer from the firm of Parchment,
Tape, and Co., as well as Wilson, had received
the same kind of treatment as had been inflicted
on the other male occupant, Thornbury. The
sagacious fellow arrived at this opinion in the
following logical manner : First of all, the two
old women had never been on ill terms with either
Thornbury or Wilson, he could not believe therefore that *they* had tied the men up; secondly, the

men could not have tied themselves up, and
therefore, as no one in the house had done it, it
seemed to follow that somebody from without
had. Nevertheless, Toby thought proper to put
the ladies to a somewhat severe cross-examination, cautioning them, after his usual manner,
that anything they might say would be taken
down in writing, and in all probability be used
against them at the trial—at what trial he could
not say. Such was Toby's mode of proceeding
when a case of importance came before him for
investigation.

Toby had almost filled his pocket book with
information, his pockets with chisels "jemmies,"
screw drivers and the like, and his handkerchief
with shoes, and by this time the shades of evening having fallen, he thought the "Talbot" was a
much safer place to be in than Heathmoor. There
was another reason why Quarterman should visit
the "Talbot;" he might hear something that would
give him another clue ; and accordingly to the
"Talbot" he went, a far more important personage

than he had been on the preceding night, for he felt he was " one of His Majesty's Government," being possessed of State secrets, upon whom it was almost treason to look. None so great in the " Talbot " that night as Toby Quarterman.

The great official walked into the room with an air of ineffable importance, and without so much as deigning to look upon the company, located himself in a huge arm chair by the hearth, where was raging and roaring the usual huge fire. He then surveyed the company, glancing mysteriously into every face, and more particularly into that of a stranger. It was not long before questions were addressed to him by butcher, baker, churchwarden, and beadle, to each of which Toby gave evasive replies.

Hopkins winked to his neighbours as he sipped his grog, intimating thereby that the time would arrive presently, and that the constable's profoundest secrets would come out.

" It's a rum business," remarked the butcher.

Smith, the village lawyer, cleared his throat

with a loud " Hem," preparatory to his deliver-
ing himself, in case he should be appealed to for
an opinion.

" 'Ave yer any clue?" enquired the beadle.

The constable slightly nodded his head, rather
by way of refusing a reply than giving one.

" Be it true they tied thic Thornbury to the
bed-posts?" asked Hopkins.

" That's about it?" said Quarterman.

" And thic Wilson?"

" The same," said the official, " and the gen'le-
man who were ere last night."

" Did em take anythink?" asked the butcher.

" Every mortal thing that ands could lift," said
the constable, who found the storm of questions
too thick to evade.

Smith hemmed again, for he was very anxious
to be asked his opinion.

" What did 'em took?" asked the beadle.
" Was there any plates?"

" Don't know yet," replied Quarterman ; "there
was a kind of box on legs—what do you call it?

—that was rumly carved; a oak thing. Great store ad been set by it, and it ad never been opened since Mrs. Hindley come to the place, for it seems the key were lost. Lor! what is the name? There *is* some name for it."

" It's *felony*," said Smith.

" 'Taint that," said Quarterman; " stands on four legs."

" You means the *dorg*," said the butcher.

" Psis !" exclaimed the constable; " what's the huse of talkin like that there ?"

" We used to call them things cabnets at old Sir George's," said Hopkins.

" Zactly!" said Smith, " that's what hi said."

" You never said nothing o' the sort," said the butcher, sneeringly. " You said it were *felony*."

" Be they got thic?" asked Hopkins. " I'll warrant me they'll 'ave a key that'll fit 'un."

Quarterman winked significantly.

" There's summut in it more an we knows on at present. Do yer know who that young feller was that were there last night ?"

Every eye was upon Quarterman.

"And what if we do, Master Quarterman?" demanded Hopkins.

"Who was un?" asked half a dozen voices at the same time.

"That were the werry son o' Squire Hindley," said the constable. "And now let me ax you, Master Hopkins, while I thinks of it, what time did un leave?"

Hopkins smiled as he repeated the question—

"What time did un leave, constable? I'll be d———d if I loaked at clock."

"Did ur stop here all night?"

"Ur stopped here till un went away, and I bleeve thee did, too."

"I sees the drift of it," interposed Smith. "You are quite right, Quarterman."

"Right!" exclaimed Hopkins, "and so be I, baint I? But what be thic pocket-book to do wi it?"

"Do you know where he's gone to?" asked the constable.

"I must be a purty feller, sure," answered Hopkins, "to ask my customers who they be, what time they go, and where be gwine to."

"I must have you afore the magistrate," said the man of authority; "but hap you'll answer me this—is un here now?"

"I tells you what it be, master constable," replied Hopkins, "my trade here be sellin' good grog, and smokin' a pleasant pipe; as for who be who, or where be where, I takes no heed, so thee 'dst better shut up pocket-book, and open thic bundle for sake o' showin' the company what be in it, for I've a notion thee be got some o' the tools o' last night's work. What be thic, a jemmy, stickin' out o' thic pocket?'"

"Never mind," said the constable, thrusting it further into his capacious coat pocket, in spite of the demands from all parts of the room for a sight of it.

"It's more than I dares do," said Quarterman. "I comes for noos, not to give it. I merely wants to know what time the young feller left."

"You see," said Smith, " a burgalary have been committed; the law have been broken, and the hoffender have to be brought to justice."

" Zactly," said Quarterman.

" Your suspicions, it seem—hem! rest upon a certain—".

" There, that'll do," said the butcher, " master constable knowed that afore.   If you can tell im who did it it'll be worth hearin'.   Do you know anything about it?"

" Hem!" said Smith. " Mind, sir, what you're a saying."

" I hear thic Thornbury wur most owdashusly wailed," said Hopkins.

" He were," said the constable.   " They tied one leg to one post, and the t'other to t'other."

" And how did the women get on?" asked another.

" Better; they took no hurt only the fright; but I 'bleeve they was most frittened to death."

" It's a strange thing," remarked Smith, " that they should ha' been so anxious for the cabinet."

" Yes; and if you know'd all you'd say so," said Quarterman. " Once more, Master Hopkins, when did young Hindly leave?"

" By the mail last night," answered the host; " but, the devil! thee don't think a man would rob his own house, do thee? How would that be, Master Smith, burgalary?"

"You see," said Smith, " hall the circumstances are werry strange; here's a young man comes ere hunexpected, hall of a sudden, goes to take possession of somebody's ouse, are refused en- trance—"

" Threatens to 'ave the werry cabinet," said Quarterman.

" Never!" exclaimed half a dozen voices.

" Yes," said Quarterman, " and atween me and you, Master Hopkins, were seen wi' some gipsies on the common only the werry night afore last. I tell you what, if that there young man wur here I should take 'im up."

" Justified!" said Smith.

" I tell thee what," said Hopkins, " it seem to

me you ought to be off arter the gipsies at once, and take 'em all up, the whole pack of 'em. I hears there's bin a pretty sight of 'em hereaway this last month. You ought to take 'em all up."

"I means to have 'em," said Quarterman, a slight shudder passing through his frame as he spoke.

And with this public awowal of his intention, he struck his glass on the table as a signal for more grog.

The conversation was prolonged to a late hour, much speculation indulged in as to the probability of a discovery, and many arguments were used against the guilt of Edgar. The gallant Quarterman grew more and more vehement in his avowal to apprehend the whole gang of gipsies as soon as he could obtain a warrant for that purpose.

CHAPTER VI.

SUPERIOR PERSONS.

In order to make the reader acquainted with the circumstances attending Mrs. Wilmington's and Lizzy's departure from the neighbourhood of Raymonds, it is necessary to take up the narrative from the time of Edgar's setting out for the metropolis.

It will be remembered that Mrs. Wilmington, at the time young Hindly fell in love with her daughter, was living on the estate of Squire Walters; a little cottage at the outskirts of the mag-

nificent demesne of Burwell, and adjoining that of
Raymond's was her abode; in fact, was exactly
on the boundary of each, for a public way being
claimed between the two estates, which both
owners were anxious to close, the cottage had
been built ostensibly as a lodge, but with the real
intention that its occupier should preclude travellers from insisting on their right of passage. It
was the duty, therefore, of Mrs. Wilmington to
keep the gate closed against all persons who were
not fully cognizant of their right, and to let those
only pass through whom it was hardly safe to
deny.

The two estates lying thus in proximity, it was
the anxious wish of Squire Walters to unite them
under one ownership by a marriage of his daughter with the only son of his neighbour. The
marriage contract had been carefully drawn, not
only to effect this object, but also to confer upon
him (Walters) the absolute title during his life.

A slight misunderstanding, however, on the
part of one of the parties principally concerned

in the matter, namely, Edgar, somewhat inter-
fered with the accomplishment of the well-in-
tended object of the two squires.

Country places never keep secrets, and the love
affair between Edgar and Lizzy was not long in
reaching the ears of Squire Walters. Thornbury
being at that time his trusty gamekeeper, and
the only man who was allowed to appropriate the
squire's rabbits and game—in fact, the only man
who was privileged to rob him—confided to his master one day the fact of having seen Master Hindly
with his arm round Lizzy Wilmington's waist.
This little "passage of arms" was the more dreadful to a person so proper as Thornbury, in consequence of his longing to perform the same act
whenever his good qualities should obtain for him
the coveted privilege.

Thornbury's word with Squire Walters was
almost sacred. Many had been the poacher that
his unsupported evidence had sent to prison; indeed, upon his testimony alone the old lady be-

fore mentioned had been convicted of stealing a
turnip, for which devilish offence the other magistrate had sent her to prison.

Thornbury was annoyed, as a matter of course,
that being so confidential an adviser of Walters,
he should be snubbed by any one in an inferior
position, and was at a loss to account for the
haughty manner in which Lizzy always resented
what she ought to have considered the most wonderful condescension on his part. He watched the
cottage hour by hour, and at last, being about to
take his farewell of Raymond, Edgar became less
guarded in his visits to the object of his affections. So the matter was discovered. Thornbury's revengeful spirit was aroused, and he endeavoured to magnify the affair into a crime.

The squire stamped, took two or three pinches
of snuff, and swore an oath against the offending
girl. The next business was to write to Edgar,
but the messenger returned with the note, saying
that he had quitted his father's roof, and that his

address was unknown. But Thornbury had already made Squire Hindly acquainted with the affair.

The presumption of Lizzy was too much for Mr. Walters; accordingly, without delay, he summoned her to his presence, the message being conveyed by Thornbury.

As Lizzy entered the library of the magistrate there was a calm, graceful dignity in her demeanour which accorded well with the beauty and elegance of her person. She was dressed somewhat, perhaps, beyond her station, but with such neatness as defied criticism. A slight tinge of colour gave an ineffable charm to a face that seemed to beam with more than mortal beauty; her large expressive blue eyes sparkled with a radiance that illumined her whole form, while a look of anxiety lent an interesting expression to her beautiful features.

The squire regarded her for a few moments from his large oaken library chair without deigning to offer her a seat, or even to recognise her with a nod of condescension such as he usually bestowed upon persons beneath him. It was evident that his eye was smitten with the charms of his lovely visitor, as the pen which he was using fell from his fingers, and he surveyed her with a glance that bespoke at once admiration and anger.

"Wilmington," he said, after a pause, intended for the abashment of his visitor, "what is this I hear of you?"

Lizzy stood as if amazed for an instant, but without losing her self-possession, replied—

"I do not know, sir."

"Not know!" exclaimed the magistrate. "Then I will tell you; but first let me ask if you know who you are, and what position you occupy in my establishment?"

"Your questions surprise me, sir; but if I appear before you as a criminal I should have had a more legal summons, and it would have been for my accusers to prefer their charge, if they had one against me."

"Of course you are *very* innocent," said Walters; "but presently we shall understand each other better. In your girlish innocence you may be ignorant that there is any distinction between right and wrong. Is that so?"

Lizzy looked with a glance of contempt at her interrogator, and remained silent.

"Perhaps you are aware," continued Walters, "that there is such a person as Mr. Edgar Hindly?"

Lizzy made a slight inclination of her head, while a deep flush suffused her countenance.

"Is that so?" asked Walters.

"Your question, sir," replied Lizzy, "scarcely demands an answer."

"But *I* demand one," said the squire, haughtily. "I say do you know such a gentleman as Mr. Edgar Hindly?"

"I answer, sir, but without acknowledging any obligation to do so, yes."

"Don't be impudent," said Walters; "it is not for those who live in my service to contemn

their benefactor, although sometimes the atten-
tions paid by fine gentlemen give dependants the
airs of ladies. I hear you have been accustomed
to receive visits from the gentleman, and that on
my premises. Is that so?"

"I do not understand you, sir," replied Lizzy;
"but if your question means that I have been
guilty of anything that does not become maiden
propriety, I tell you plainly that I regard your
question as an insult, and your informant, who
ever he may be, is a base coward."

"Even if it were Squire Hindly himself I suppose?"

"Even if it were the king himself," replied
Lizzy.

"You have read novels to some purpose I see,"
said Walters: "and your language is certainly
fine for a rustic damsel whose mother is my lodge-
keeper, so is your dress somewhat grand for your
position."

"Mr. Walters, I wish you good-morning," said
the offended girl; "it is unmanly of you to put

these insults upon me because my station is beneath your own; but humble as I am I can feel insults, even from *superiors*, though I may not have the power to punish them."

"Stay," said Walters; "your conduct in my presence accords with the character I have heard of you. And now understand me, I shall suffer no one to remain on my estate who receives visits at all from gentlemen whose station in society ought to convince a right-minded girl that their intentions cannot be right."

"Do I understand, sir, that you accuse Mr. Hindly of dishonourable intentions? if so, his defence must rest in abler hands than those of a helpless girl."

As Lizzy spoke the tears shone in her beautiful eyes, but with a strong effort she repressed the emotion which she could not entirely conceal.

"Really," said Mr. Walters, "your language is so much more like that of a fine lady than of a simple country girl, that I must needs call you *miss*."

" I am not the simple country girl which your simplicity believes me," said Lizzy; "and if I may be allowed the same freedom of speech, I must say that your language so little becomes the lips of a gentleman that, but for your position, I would drop the *sir* in addressing you."

" You are an impudent wench," said Walters, half-mad with rage, "and but that your sex protects you—"

" I almost wonder that it does," said Lizzy.

" Listen !" said Walters. " You are aware that Mr. Hindly was engaged to my daughter."

" It is nothing to me, sir," replied the unhappy girl.

" No ; to such as you honour and chastity—"

" Dare to insult me further, and even you, great as you esteem yourself, shall rue it. I came hither in obedience to your message ; but it was not to endure insults, which you would not dare offer if Mr. Hindly were here to resent them. You are a *coward*, sir."

Walters grated his teeth, and muttered a curse ;

his eyes shot flashes of indignation, and he looked rather like an enraged demon than a human being. Some moments elapsed, and Lizzy was about to withdraw, when, assuming an air of more composure, the offended magistrate again addressed her—

"You are rash, Wilmington, and offend your best friends. I would ask you—but take a seat."

"No, no," said Lizzy.

"I would ask you," continued Walters, "if there is any engagement between you and Edgar Hindly?"

"I challenge your right to question me," said Lizzy.

"He has left his father's roof under circumstnces which leave us ample room for suspicion."

"Suspicion!" said Lizzy; "then pray, sir, have the courage to mention your suspicions to Edgar himself. I have no doubt he will answer you; for myself, I do not understand you."

"In what school, pray, were you educated?" asked Walters, "and what were your parents' antecedents before you came under my notice?"

"I believe my mother was presented to you by two lady friends of hers who had known her in better circumstances."

"I had forgotten," said Walters. "Yes, yes, your father was—"

"I don't know," said the girl; "but if you please I will receive your commands, and take my leave."

"I believe," said Walters, "there was at one time some partiality between you and my gamekeeper, Thornbury, who, by-the-bye, is an admirable young fellow. Was that so?"

Lizzy's look of contempt made the old man pause.

"Nay," said he, "you need not fly off so; it's a pity your ideas are not confined to your station; there are more loves that beauty unmakes than makes; but I believe it was so, was it not?"

"I refuse to answer," said Lizzy.

" You refuse to confess," said he ; " well, well, that's as good as a confession at any rate. Come, we shall understand each other presently. I suppose, bad as you think me, you will not deem me much the worse for offering you five hundred pounds ?"

Lizzy was somewhat bewildered ; and for the moment she doubted the man's sanity.

" I see," he continued, " you don't understand me. I mean this—you have been grossly used by that young scapegrace Hindly. Is that so?"

Lizzy said nothing.

" I see this ill-assorted amour must come to a termination ; you are an injured girl."

Lizzy's feelings were divided between anger and contempt.

" Injured !" said she, " in what way ?"

" At least to your reputation," said Walters.

" And because my reputation then, is, as you term it, injured you will give me five hundred pounds ?"

" You are a foolish girl," replied Walters. " I

would like to see you fairly settled, and to be plain with you—Thornbury is fond of you,—and to make you happy and comfortable I will give you what I say."

Lizzy laughed ; the idea was too absurd to call forth an expression of anger.

Walters looked at her for some moments, utterly unable to understand her humour.

"Thornbury," he said, "will make a good husband."

"Then I would advise you to secure him for your own daughter," answered Lizzy, "for if all be true that I have heard, good husbands are a rare commodity."

Walters' face was flushed with indignation, and as he looked at the proud girl his eyes were bloodshot with rage, and his whole countenance was covered with confusion.

"You saucy, impudent wench !" he exclaimed, "how dare you thus insult me ? I have a mind to—to—to—"

Anger forbade his finishing the sentence.

Lizzy was unmoved by his awful visage, and rather enjoyed his confused demeanour.

" You are the most ungrateful creature," he said; " I will have no more to do with you. Pride has already been the foundation of your ruin ; you'll come to want and shame as sure as your name is Wilmington; but I pity you, because you have had no sterner hand to control you than a foolish and indulgent mother, whom I shall send about her business presently."

" Good-morning, sir," said Lizzy.

" Stay ! " roared Walters, " I have another word yet. You have refused my offer; but you have not cleared your character, mind, and I will have no such creatures on my estate."

Lizzy had already quitted the room, and the last part of this generous speech was unheard.

Passing hastily through the hall, and thence into the grounds, she encountered Thornbury, who, with an eye to the proffered sum—for the matter had already been arranged between him and his master—was waiting to hear the result

of the interview.   He stood right in the pathway
of the agitated girl, who, without so much as
deigning to look at him, attempted to pass.

"Stay, my pretty queen," said he, smiling.
Lizzy, however, said nothing.

"What have I done, then, Lizzy?"

"Let me pass."

"Pass, eh?" replied Thornbury; "have yer
grown so proud, then, over your new lover? mark
me, there's little good comes o' genlemen's
wisits to poor gals; if master been rating you it's
no reason why you should be ont wi' me."

Lizzy made an attempt to pass without replying to the remark; but Thornbury sidled somewhat, and again intercepted her path.

"Look," said he, "we must be darned fools,
Lizzy, not to take so capital a orfer; I'll warrant
thee Edgar 'll never come down with half so much;
and it's well to get your krackter back.   Why,
arf the gals would go mad at such a charnce;
come, let's ave a better face on it."

"Wretch!" exclaimed the girl; "desist from

your loathsome interference. I would you were a reptile in form as you are in nature."

"Ha! ha!" said Thornbury, laughing with fiendish triumph, "we shall see, my proud wench —you carrys a big sail, but big sails sometimes makes shipwrecks. Do yer ear me? you'll never get such a price for your putty face, and beauty, you knows, won't keep. Come, say you'll think about un."

Once more she endeavoured to pass, and Thornbury was about to take her hand, when she looked at him with eyes that expressed the contempt she felt.

"Dare to lay a finger on me!" she exclaimed, "and as Heaven is my maker I will make you repent it!"

The look was too much for the dastardly spirit of Thornbury; his face coloured, his lips quivered, while his hand dropped by his side as though he dreaded immediate vengeance.

"Go," said he; "the next time I make yer a orfer you'll take it. You're only a gentleman's plaything; but go and tell your mother the news—ha! ha!"

Lizzy's eyes filled with tears as she hurried from the cowardly keeper, disdaining to reply to his insults, or even to glance upon him the contempt which she felt.

As she hastened towards the cottage she wondered why it was that she should be the victim of such oppressors? Her conduct was irreproachable, save that she had suffered herself to love one who was so far above her; if that were a crime she was guilty.

And in the bitterness of her heart she wished that she might forget Edgar. Fatal of all moments was that when her eyes first encountered his handsome form. Why did he disguise his true position, and represent himself as her equal in station, and why had she been so blind as not to perceive in his dignified deportment, and his elegant language, one superior to the person he had represented himself to be? But he had won her love, and if Edgar could never fulfil his promise there was not another upon earth that could be placed in his stead. If she had been guilty of a crime, a life of disappointment and loneliness would be her penance.

With these reflections she arrived at her mother's door. The old lady was wondering what could be the meaning of the summons—whether ill or good might result from it she was at a loss to divine; the sorrowful countenance of her daughter, however, put an end to her speculations.

" Lizzy, what has happened ? — what has happened ?"

Lizzy threw herself into a chair, and covering her face with her hands, gave way to the grief that was weighing down her heart.

" What is it, my child, tell me ?"

" Oh, mother, do not ask me !"

" What has he said to you, my dear ?"

" It is all through me, mother," replied Lizzy, but her feelings prevented for awhile a further explanation.

" What is through you, child ?"

" We must leave the cottage," said Lizzy, " and all because of poor Edgar. Oh, mother, I wish I had never seen him."

" Stay," said Mrs. Wilmington, "I do not regret, even though I shall be homeless. I have news for this proud magistrate one day that will make his ears tingle."

" What news, mother ?"

"Ask nothing, my child, but remember my words when the time comes. What did he say ? "

" He told me my character was ruined, and a great deal more which I cannot repeat, and dare not remember, for it would drive me mad; and he offered me five hundred pounds to marry that wretch Thornbury."

" He did," said Mrs. Wilmington. " Then the old fox —— ah, no, that cannot be—that cannot be."

And the mother paused as though she was weighing in her mind some doubtful point—her expressions, indeed, were spoken rather to herself than her daughter.

"And what else? Did you answer him promptly, and, as I hope, with disdain?"

"I did," said Lizzy, "so much so that I am afraid I increased the mischief; and he told me I was a mighty fine spoken lady, or something to that effect, and asked me who was my father, and where—"

"Ah!" interrupted the old lady, "did he ask you that? And because you refused his offer we are to leave, are we?"

"So he said," answered Lizzy. "Oh, mother, my heart is almost broken to think of your being homeless."

"My child," said Mrs. Wilmington, "God who provides for the ravens will not neglect us. I have struggled these many years, trusting in Heaven, where the star of my comfort shines. Ever since you were a babe, such as I could lay in my bosom, I have been a wanderer, destitute of what the world calls comfort, but still supplied with daily bread from His hands who can feed the hungry in the wilderness. My girl, if you knew how to trust implicitly in Heaven, you would not have fears to make you sad."

"But, mother, you have never told me that great secret which you have so often promised I should know, about my father. When he asked me who was my father I thought a great deal of your long widowhood. The question sounded so strange you cannot imagine."

"My poor child," said Mrs. Wilmington, " I will one day tell you, but not now ; he was a soldier, and was said to have been killed in battle."

"But did you never know ?" asked Lizzy.

"Don't ask me now, Lizzy."

The poor old lady could not suppress the tears that started to her eyes. The subject was one of so painful a nature that Lizzy seldom ventured to pursue her enquiries, her mother invariably evading her questions, or turning the conversation into a different channel.

At this moment the door was opened, without the civility of a preliminary knock, and Mrs. Walters haughtily entered the room. She was a tall, dark, sallow-complexioned woman of about fifty, whose scornful demeanour lent even an additional severity to her stern and unlovely features.

Lizzy offered her a seat, with a grace that contrasted strangely with the unpolite manner of its refusal.

"Wilmington," said she, "we did not expect when we took you into our establishment, that you would abuse our charity."

"Charity!" exclaimed Mrs. Wilmington; "I do not understand you; perhaps your ladyship will be good enough to explain."

"And the *abuse* of it," said Lizzy.

"You are a pert wench!" exclaimed Lady Walters, "and the sooner you leave these premises the better; it's a disgrace to the establishment to have you here."

"Pardon me, Lady Walters," said Mrs. Wilmington, " but so long as we are within these walls I shall take care that my daughter receives no insults even from you; she has been grossly abused already by—by Sir Robert, and—"

"Infamous woman!" said Lady Walters, "what do you mean? my husband has been generous—nay, he has acted almost the part of a father to your daughter, and thus you reward him. Base creatures, leave at once; I came to offer terms; but you are unworthy—go!"

"Thank you," said Mrs. Wilmington; "we *may* meet again, and then Lady Walters will know herself better."

Her ladyship heard the remark, but made no reply, and stepping into her pony carriage drove hastily away.

CHAPTER VII.

A TRUE-HEARTED WOMAN.

IT was on the following morning that a lady of
very different character knocked lightly at the
cottage door. Lizzy and her mother were engaged in packing up their few articles of furni-
ture and apparel preparatory to their departure.
Lizzy glanced from the window to see who the
unexpected visitor was, and immediately a deep
blush suffused her countenance. She trembled,
and was too agitated to open the door.

" What ails you, child?" asked Mrs. Wilmington.

" It's Mrs. Hindly!" exclaimed Lizzy; " but I have done no wrong, and—no, I will not avoid her.   Open the door, mother dear."

Mrs. Wilmington admitted the visitor.

" Good-morning, Wilmington—Lizzy."

And she immediately seized the girl's hand, as if to assure her that the fears which were manifested on her countenance were entirely groundless.

" I have not come to reproach you," said she, "far from it ; but I am not unconscious of the malicious rumours that are in circulation respecting you, equally to the hurt of your own as to my son's reputation; but let me ask you—for I will come at once to the point—has Edgar been so rash as, without means or prospects, to promise you marriage?   Nay, Lizzy, don't fear to disclose all to me.   I love him too dearly and regret his loss too deeply to be angry, much as I may reproach him for his inconsiderate haste.   Does he call you his wife? "

" No, madam," said Lizzy, bursting into tears, and sobbing violently, " nor could I ever aspire to such a position."

" But why, my child ? " asked Mrs. Hindly. " Did you never encourage his addresses ? "

" It was before I knew his true rank," said Lizzy.

" What ! " exclaimed Mrs. Hindly, " did he deceive you ?—woo you under a false name ? "

" No—no," said Lizzy ; " but he did not tell me who he was until we both loved too deeply to—"

" I see," said Mrs. Hindly ; " it was unkind—ungenerous of him."

" No," answered Lizzy, " not unkind. Edgar was never unkind, save to himself; never ungenerous. Oh, madam, he is all that is noble and good. I wish he had been less considerate of my happiness, and more devoted to his own interests. Heaven must vindicate my character. O, madam, this is the cruelest of all—this false accusation."

"Time will prove," said Mrs. Wilmington ; "time will prove."

"I have come to offer you a home," said Mrs. Hindly, " a home where you shall be alike free from insult and intrusion. My estate at Heathmoor is untenanted, and you shall take possession as my housekeeper. What do you say ?"

"Generous lady!" exclaimed Lizzy ; "it is too good of you."

"God shall recompense you," said Mrs. Wilmington. "Come, Lizzy, child, no more crying ; we shall see one of these days what will transpire. Oh, Mrs. Hindly, I would like to tell you a secret that —but no, not yet—not yet, even to you."

"Does it concern my son ?" demanded the lady.

Mrs. Wilmington shook her head, and a smile like that of intense pleasure lit up her countenance.

"Yet you shall hear it one day."

"And why not now ?"

"Do, mother, let us know—let us know it ; you have so long promised."

" When you come to Heathmoor, madam,"
said Mrs. Wilmington, " I will tell you all."

Mrs. Hindly felt all her woman's curiosity, but
forbore further questions on the subject, merely
remarking that she was glad her offer pleased,
and that she should take an early opportunity of
visiting them. Turning to Lizzy, she seemed to
regard her with a look that spoke at once admiration and affection. What there was in her
countenance that riveted her gaze it was impossible to say, but her whole manner spoke plainly
enough that it was no wonder so much beauty
should have won from her son so much admiration. Romantic in disposition as Edgar was, and
with a highly imaginative mind, she would have
been the rather astonished if his powers of fancy
had not invested the girl before her with the
charms of a goddess. But probably there was
another feeling akin to curiosity, as Mrs. Hindly
contemplated the ladylike demeanour of Lizzy,
which seemed to suggest that she was not the
low-born girl which her position indicated. How-

ever, this was also the effect of her imagination, if we may ascribe to fancy that which is sometimes more justly due to the judgment.

There was in the circumstances of Mrs. Wilmington a mystery which had sometimes given a spur to speculation, but which, now that she had seen her daughter, and had listened to her language, led her to the conclusion that she might be an unfortunate gentlewoman in the disguise of adversity.

Wishing them both a hearty good-bye, Mrs. Hindly took her departure, giving the necessary directions for the journey, and a letter which she had prepared for the occasion.

" What," asked Lizzy, " can be the meaning of all this ? Oh, mother, I am as full of joy as I was an hour since of misery."

" Yes," answered Mrs. Wilmington, " our joys are generally pretty close on the heels of our sorrows ; but I tell you, child, I have never yet doubted Providence."

" But what is it, mother, you have to tell ? Is

there a mystery hanging over my birth? It seems to me that we are not altogether like other poor people; you know more than others of our class; your conversation is not like theirs, nor are your manners. I have noticed this. And then, again, you have taught me. Tell me, mother, this, if nothing more, were you ever in better circumstances? Were you never as great a lady as Mrs. Hindly?"

"My child," said Mrs. Wilmington, "the time is not far distant when you shall learn all; at present it is my wish to remain silent on the subject."

"Oh, mother, if Edgar could know that—that you were, that is, had been in a high position."

"And what then, my child? Do you think *I* could recognise a love that was based upon such a foundation? No. He has had a fair opportunity of estimating your worth; if he does not love you as you are, I will never furnish him with knowledge that will be likely to influence him. You are as dear to me, Lizzy, as though we moved amid circles of fashion and splendour. Edgar is not more worthy of you because he belongs to a family of rank. I have lived long enough, and am sufficiently experienced to know, that virtue and honour belong to no particular class, and that marriages based upon expediency or ambition are not productive of happiness?"

"But were you not surprised that Mrs. Hindly should treat us with so much kindness? I'm sure I quite dreaded to meet her."

"And why, my dear? I hope that face will never blush to behold a living being. *Dread* to meet a fellow-creature! No mortal eye hath ever looked me down yet. The owl may blink at the twinkling star; but the eagle faces the sun."

"But I felt guilty, mother — guilty of her misery. But for me Edgar might still have been the pride and sunlight of her heart. O yes, *I am* guilty of all this unhappiness."

"Mrs. Hindly does not think you guilty, or her heart must be more than human to show us so much kindness."

"She is like Edgar," said Lizzy, "as much in goodness and generosity as in features. Oh, how like him she was as she offered us the home at Heathmoor. But she will be dying to know your secret."

Mrs. Wilmington smiled, and turned to complete the preparations for their journey. But Lizzy's heart was so full of joy at the unexpected pleasure that for awhile she forgot her grief for Edgar's loss. There were intervals, however, when it would force itself upon her heart, and when the recollection of former days, never to be recalled, shaded her mind. Mrs. Hindly's kindness was a mystery to her, and in spite of her wish to flatter herself that she was an object of that lady's esteem, as she had been of her son's affection, an icy thrill darted through her heart as she exclaimed—

"I have it—I have it now, mother."

"Have what, my dear?"

"I know why Mrs. Hindly likes us so much;

it is because I refused to marry Edgar; you know he *did* offer me marriage."

"I have not so read Mrs. Hindly's feelings," answered Mrs. Wilmington. "I believe she esteems you on that account; but the refusal makes her think you the more worthy to accept."

"No, mother, not worthy. I never could be worthy of Edgar; my love was a mistake—a wretched mistake. I could never move in his position, whatever the marriage rite might make us. I wish that those months might be blotted out of my life. I can never love another who is not his equal, and his equal I shall never see. I shall not be able to requite so much devotion. Oh Heaven! when I refused his last offer my heart seemed to break; I felt that I was turning from me all that had made life lovely."

"And did you reject him, Lizzy, entirely?"

"And for ever," answered the unhappy girl. "How could I venture?—he, ambitious, proud, talented; I, a poor, dowerless, uneducated girl! Could I ever have moved amid the circle of fine ladies with whom his future home will be dazzled? No, I must bury my love in my own heart, and be a mourner for ever. If Edgar could have lived in humble competence; but no—no, though he were willing to sacrifice his prospects for me, I would never—never curb his ambition. I could be the starlight of his home, but not the shadow. But it's past, mother, and if I could but forget him, I would not care though the grave—"

"Lizzy!" exclaimed Mrs. Wilmington, who was alarmed at the wild tone and manner of her daughter, and feared a relapse into the despondency which, since Edgar's departure, had taken possession of her. "Lizzy, child, do not talk so, I thought you were firmer of purpose. Think you no one has suffered losses but you? Look at me, an old woman on the verge of sixty, and at thirty with all the bloom, though I say it myself, of your own girlhood, and with more than your hopes, I bore a shock such as would have broken a heart of adamant. You have done well in all that has passed, and your conduct does you credit. Look up to God, and He who knows your faithfulness will not leave it unrewarded."

Lizzy listened as the tears streamed from her eyes, and heaving a sigh, she turned to arrange her books and papers.

Mrs. Hindly, meanwhile, had returned to her house; but the pleasure she felt in having performed so worthy an act, was damped on her arrival. Mr. Hindly met her with a gloomy countenance, and listened to her account of what she had done with anything but a feeling of pleasure.

"You are bent upon ruining me," he said, sternly; "in the name of heaven how can you offer protection to such people?"

"Such people, my dear," repeated Mrs. Hindly. "They are not such people as rumour represents them, and if through the folly of Edgar they are deprived of a home, it is no reason why we should suffer them to want while we have the means of rescuing them."

"Do as you will," said the stern husband. "I shall be glad to rid the village of such characters; they have brought disgrace and ruin upon us. What can Sir Robert think?"

"Think!" said Mrs. Hindly. "I know not what he may think, but his conduct is unjust, cruel, and heartless; for my own part, I would rather that Edgar should marry that girl than Lucy."

"Enough!" answered Hindly; "I have done with Edgar for ever; let him follow his course; not one penny shall he ever receive from me."

"Mr. Hindly," said his wife, "there is something in these Wilmingtons more than their circumstances show; there is a romance connected with their history that—"

"Bah!" exclaimed Hindly; "of course there is, there always is some fine romance connected with a peasant girl who falls in love with a gentlemen. They are simply artful, designing creatures, who can invent any tale to impose upon a credulous ear. Don't tell me anything of it. Give them your house if you like; it's not long since this same romantic heroine was in love with Thornbury."

"Never," said Mrs. Hindly; "such a nature could no more love a man like him than a lamb would bleat after a hungry wolf."

"You have," said Hindly, "countenanced the proceedings which you should have resented with scorn. We are simply ruined, that's all. If Walters calls in his money he must foreclose, and we must become his tenants. However, I don't care. Let it be so; but never shall Edgar receive a welcome or assistance from me."

"Nay," said Mrs. Hindley; "do not speak so; he is our only child."

"But as stubborn a churl as ever woman gave birth to; curse him."

Mrs. Hindly burst into tears, and flinging herself at her husband's feet, begged him to retract his words.

"Never," said Hindly; "he is unworthy of my blessing. Let him take my curse as his legacy; it is all I shall ever leave him."

"God forgive you," said his wife, "for cursing your own flesh and blood."

"If he were my right hand I would cut it off," said Hindly. "How dare he contemn my advice? Has he lived longer in the world than I, that he should know better, and presume to dictate? No, Amelia, I will have none of your caresses, and I wish I had had the last of them before he was born. I tell you we are ruined, and here comes Walters himself. In Heaven's name don't let him see you."

Hindly had scarcely spoken before Sir Robert was announced, and in a few moments, agitated, and with a somewhat confused air, he entered the apartment.

"Hindly, how are you? Mrs. Hindly—"

He checked himself.

"Mrs. Hindly," said her husband, "is grieved

beyond endurance over this unhappy affair. Walters, I am almost distracted myself. What's to be done ?"

" I have had the impudent wench before me," said Sir Robert ; " as saucy a jade as ever ruffled it before her betters. I was never so abused in all my life."

" There !" said Hindly, looking towards his wife, " what did 1 tell you ?"

Mrs. Hindly made no reply, preferring to be a listener to the revelation that Walters was about to make.

" I have discharged them," said Walters ; " and what is more, offered the girl five hundred pounds to start with if she liked to marry Thornbury, who is, as you know, as worthy a fellow as ever wore shoes."

" And she refused ?" said Hindly.

" Yes ; and with a saucy manner, as I might have expected from such a ——"

Mrs. Hindly's presence forbade the expression which was on Sir Robert's lips.

" But we shall bring them to it yet. Let her

get out of my keeping, and poverty will bring her to it. It's a rare antidote for this romantic pride, you know."

"True," said Hindly, "but the plan's frustrated already, for Mrs. Hindly has offered them a home at Heathmoor. I'm awfully wild about it, I am."

"Were they ten times my enemies," said Mrs. Hindly, "I would not let them want bread. My housekeeper at Heathmoor is about to leave, and the poor old woman shall take her place. It's hard, Sir Robert, for a person of her years to be turned adrift upon the world without a home; and Heaven knows what any of us may want."

Walters looked annoyed and somewhat angry at this intelligence, for he had hoped, as he said, to drive Lizzy to accept his proposition by the helplessness of her situation, cowardly and fiendish as the design was.

"Do you not think," said he, addressing Mrs. Hindly, "that the better course was the one I

attempted ?   If we could marry the girl comfortably there would be an end of the matter."

"I do not see," answered Mrs. Hindly, "that
we need trouble ourselves about her marriage;
the unhappy affair between Edgar and her has
terminated, and perhaps, after all, it will turn out
for the best.   He couldn't do better than leave
for a time."

"But he will know—"

"He will know nothing of her," said Mrs.
Hindly; "and, indeed, I believe it is all at an
end.   It was a foolish freak."

At this moment Mrs. Hindly's absence was
necessary, on account of the arrival of a visitor
whom she had appointed to see, and the two
magistrates were left to discuss the matter between themselves.   Walters felt his advantage
over his debtor, and was determined to avail himself of it, while Hindly had no scruple about
yielding to his suggestions.

"This, perhaps," said Sir Robert, "is a fortu-
nate movement on the part of Mrs. Hindly; for

if we can send Thornbury to keep this girl company, he may in time bring her to his terms. He's devilish fond of her; at all events, the bait's too dazzling for refusal; it's a devilish nuisance."

"How is Lizzy?" asked Hindly.

"She has not left her room since Edward's departure," replied Walters. "It's a bad business; a d—— bad business."

"Edgar has been entrapped," said Hindly. "You know, so far as his intention of marrying the girl was concerned, it was out of the question. But we know, Walters, what these matters are. A pretty face would never bear long looking at, would it?"

Walters smiled, but there was a twitch of the countenance that was not altogether consistent with his smile.

Hindly, in spite of the good feeling which had so long subsisted between the families, could not but look upon Sir Robert's offer to Mrs. Wilmington as something extraordinary and unaccountable; yet, such is the power of self-flattery, that

he ascribed even this to the high opinion which
Walters retained of his undeserving son. Notwithstanding the obligations he was under to the
baronet, he could not but believe that the ad-
vantages of the projected marriage were rather
on the side of Walters than himself. However,
the matter for the present was finally arranged,
and, without Mrs. Hindly's knowledge, the re-
doubtable Thornbury was to take up his abode
at Heathmoor in the capacity of keeper—a situation which that worthy fellow was by no means
likely to refuse; especially as part of the game
he would have to keep was so much to his fancy,
while the powers of pilfering the rest would be
in exact proportion to his disposition to avail
himself of them.

CHAPTER VIII.

A SHADOW OF PAST EVENTS.

NOTWITHSTANDING the scheme which was thus devised for carrying out the laudable intentions of Walters, it was found expedient to postpone its execution. Several months were therefore allowed to elapse before it was again mentioned. At length, however, Thornbury was despatched upon his important mission. One reason for the delay was the project of Mrs. Hindly's visit to Heathmoor, which took place some months after Mrs. Wilmington and Lizzy had gone to live there.

When she returned to Raymonds there was a marked change in her manner when the Wilmington's were mentioned, and her infatuation, as her husband termed it, for those people, seemed more rooted than ever. The subject was never pleasing to the ears of Hindly, but with a perverse propensity to suggest topics of an unwelcome nature, he frequently spoke of the splendid *protegée* of his wife. The idea of her cherishing a friendship for a girl who had been the ruin of his hopes was the source of continual bickerings, of taunting irony on his part, and of many tears on that of his gentle and amiable wife.

"I know," said she, shortly after her return from Heathmoor, "that you accuse me of encouraging Edgar's attachment to Lizzy Wilmington, but nothing was ever farther from my heart."

"And yet you must needs provide a home for them, where, for anything I know, this clandestine business may be carried on."

"It is not so," said Mrs. Hindly. "There has

been no correspondence between them; the affair has been entirely broken off; but this, let me tell you, dear, Wilmington is not what *you* think she is, not the person Sir Robert thinks her."

" Still a heroine," said Hindly jeeringly. " Methinks I would like to see her then without her mask."

" You may one day," said Mrs. Hindly. " I have heard a tale from her mother's lips that would fill the newspapers were it known. Fiction is once more outdone by fact."

" My dear," said Hindly, " I thought you were beyond the jugglery of these women who live by tales of mystery. I'll warrant she has been a gipsy fortune teller before now, and, by the way, her appearance smacked somewhat of the romantic, I remember."

" What was there of the romantic?" asked Mrs. Hindly.

" I remember," said Hindly, " she was recommended to me by the vicar, at the entreaty of two ancient spinsters, who had been in India, and who, it seems, took marvellous interest in this wandering woman. It was a plausible tale, if I remember rightly. Her husband was killed in the Peninsula. Now, it strikes me that those spinsters were sheer impostors."

" And the vicar, my dear ?"

" Well, like the generality of his cloth, he was easily imposed upon by any one who had hypocrisy enough.   But let us have the strange tale."

" I have promised not to divulge it," said Mrs. Hindly.

" That is exactly what I expected, and confirms my opinion. These lying jades always adopt that sort of device for their protection ; so it must never be told, eh ?"

" You will have the means of judging one day," said Mrs. Hindly.   " It's a pity you did not see this girl yourself."

" To what purpose?" angrily demanded Hindly —" to judge of her fitness for my daughter-in-law ? You may have her for your friend if you like, but neither she nor her paramour is any of mine. I'll have no such creatures in my keeping."

" You wrong her ?" said Mrs. Hindly.

" Not much while you have her in your stall," said Hindly. " You know the Scripture—' the ox knoweth his owner, and the ass his master's crib.' She was a poor ass, but didn't know such a mistress as you ; but I commend her for her cunning."

" She has seen better days," said Mrs. Hindly.

" And will see worse, or I mistake the horoscope," rejoined her husband. " There never was one of these upstart, malapert impostors but had ' seen better days,' had been ruined by a law suit, robbed by executors, or something else ; why, half the world has seen better days, but the sun only shines on one half at a time, and therefore the other must be in darkness. You had better tell her tale to Walters."

" He would scarcely be so incredulous as yourself," said Mrs. Hindly, " and probably you will remember what I say some day. Sir Robert will not be so doubtful or so unjust in his surmises as yourself."

"Then Walters is a greater fool than ever I thought him," said Hindly. "That's all I can say; but for me, I hate the name of Wilmington, and desire never to hear it mentioned again."

"From me you never shall," answered his wife, who resumed the book she had been reading.

This was Hindly's usual manner of finishing an altercation in which he came off second best. He chuckled, however, over the more important secret of Thornbury's departure for Heathmoor, and daily expected to hear from Walters either that the game had been fairly trapped by the crafty keeper or dislodged. To him it was the most desirable thing in the world to accomplish either. To achieve the first result would baffle any secret scheme of his son's; the second would be a triumph over his wife, for he felt that her interference in the matter was as much an assertion of her own right over his, as the result of a charitable feeling. Thornbury, at all events, would be the means of ruining the girl's prospects with his son, or her character with the world, if the latter had not already been accomplished. With these consolatory reflections he strolled down to Burwell. On his way he met Sir Robert and Lady Walters. Their conversation gave some insight into the manner of Thornbury's deportment at Heathmoor, and the success of his schemes for the first month after his arrival.

"News from Heathmoor?" asked Hindly.

" Of no importance," said Walters. " Our missionary's efforts at converting this pretty heathen are at present fruitless. He thinks, however, that she cannot hold out long."

" It would be an excellent thing for her," said Lady Walters, who, like most married ladies, was an ardent match maker.

" Of course it was a surprise to them?" said Hindly.

" So much so that the girl secluded herself for a whole week, and resented all the man's advances as insults. She's the most cunning creature I ever heard of."

"And the most impertinent," said Lady Walters. "I wouldn't for the world have such people on the estate, Mr. Hindly, if my subsistence depended upon it."

"And yet," said Hindly, "she is reported to be a girl of manners beyond her station."

"Such is the effect of this education of the lower orders," answered the lady, "and this modern literature, which gives a smattering of grand manners to every wench."

"You are quite right," said Hindly, whose Tory principles were as unmistakable as those of the baronet.

"We shall hear by and bye, I dare say," rejoined Hindly. "I'm heartily sorry that my wife should have given shelter to such people, who are nothing but impostors, palming themselves upon the public as people of reduced circumstances."

"Reduced circumstances!" exclaimed her ladyship. "I am astonished at public credulity."

" Had I heard this before," said Walters, " I would have had the old woman on the rack of cross-examination. But how was this rumour circulated?"

" I believe she confessed something to my wife," said Hindly, " and by that means worked upon her sympathies, or she never could have condescended to give them shelter."

There was an expression on Sir Robert's countenance at this moment, which did not escape the observation of his wife.

" My dear," said she, " are you ill? The sun is too much for you."

" It is nothing," said Sir Robert ; a slight tremor passing through his frame as Lady Walters took his arm.

" What is it, dear?" again demanded the lady, " you are ill?"

" No, no," said Sir Robert.

" Do you know, Mr. Hindly, Sir Robert has never been himself since that girl insulted him.

You should have punished her, Robert;—but let us return."

Hindly accompanied them to the mansion, where a letter was lying, the superscription of which was that of Thornbury; but Walters felt too indisposed to attend even to an affair of such importance at that moment.

CHAPTER IX.

JUST IN TIME.

THE course of conduct which Thornbury pursued towards Lizzy on his arrival at Heathmoor was such as only a thorough paced villain could adopt. To say that he was capable of affection such as subsists in the breast of a lover, were to utter a libel upon human nature. The time might have been, in his earlier existence, when he could have regarded one so beautiful and pure with a feeling of respect and admiration, but his coarse nature was revolting even under its best aspects, and

H 5

when he received the first repulse from her re-
fined spirit, the demon of his evil genius seemed
to awake within him. He had been the terror of
every servant at Burwell, and was amazed that
Lizzy should refuse his advances. The consequence was that rumours were circulated with
respect to the Wilmingtons of a character by no
means likely to raise them in the esteem of the
family. Their removal was the consequence of
the character which Thornbury had given them.

At Heathmoor there was an excellent opportunity of persecuting the girl who had refused the
honor of his addresses, and the villain felt that he
was well protected by the hatred which Walters
bore her. To the work, then, of conquest or revenge he determined to apply himself with all
the craft and perseverance of his malignant
nature. The love of money was not without its
influence, and he felt that if he could but induce
Lizzy to consent to a marriage, his desires would
be gratified to the full. Five hundred pounds
was a fortune such as a man might do anything

to obtain—and the five hundred pounds he was determined to possess, or the wench should bitterly rue the pride which urged her to reject him.

The morning after his arrival he demanded admittance to the room which Lizzie and her mother occupied. It was refused, and Lizzy shrinking from his persecution, and dreading his ferocious nature, kept her chamber for some days.

Thornbury meanwhile kept somewhat aloof, fearing, lest by too determined an approach he might give more alarm than would further his project. Several weeks passed by, at the end of which, so secretly had Thornbury's movements been, that his presence at the Abbey was almost a matter of doubt—at all events Lizzy felt convinced that he had accepted his defeat, and had abandoned his futile projects. She therefore resolved upon a visit to the inn, a description of which has already been given, in order to ascertain if any letter had been left there to be called for.

Mrs. Hindly had thought it expedient to adopt that means of communication between her and the unfortunate girl in whom she took so deep an interest.

It is not necessary to enter again upon the scene so eventful to Edgar ; it will suffice to say that Mrs. Hopkins took at once a liking to the pretty girl, and felt great curiosity the moment she heard her ask if there was a letter " for L. W., to be called for." The letter itself for the last five days had been a source of unutterable wonderment to the landlady and Charles ; there was a romance attached to it and a lover, so the good lady asked Lizzy if she would step inside and read it.

" You be from Heathmoor," said Mrs. Hopkins.

" Yes," replied Lizzie, blushing somewhat at the boldness of the invitation.

" The lady were here some time ago," said Mrs. Hopkins, " but will thee please to step inside. Chars—Chars, here be a lady for thic letter from Heathmoor; didn't I tell thee it were so, and Chars would have it miss, it were no sich thing; but do thee step inside, miss—it must be very lonely at th' Abbey for thee."

" Beest thee from Squire Hindly's?" demanded Hopkins, as he entered at this moment; "why, bless the lady, I be old Sir—lor—lor—lor— what's his name?"

" Lor thee mean'st Sir George's, Chars."

" Ay, Sir George's bailiff years agoo," said Hopkins.

" Do you mean Sir Robert Walters?" en- quired Lizzy, "of Burwell Park, near Raymond?"

" No, no, child," answered the landlord, with his usual familiarity; "Lady Hindly's—as I call her, for she *be* a lady—Lady Hindly's father, and my wife here wur—what wur it, Nancy?—the butler I thinks."

" Get along, Chars, do; thee know'st not what thee beest talking 'bout."

" And thee wast but a poor skinny thing when I married thee, Nancy, and now look at thee; there be scarcely a butt in my cellar, but an' it were dressed in petticoats wi' a fardengale but would—"

"Get along wi' the nonsense, Charles.   Miss, theest had a long walk, and a long one before thee.   Tea is ready, and thee must take a cup wi' us."

Lizzy felt somewhat strange, not only at such unusual familiarity, but also at such unceremonious proffers of hospitality; but, although she had travelled much, she had not met with people whose manners, uncultured as they were, were yet more apparently genuine.   There was good nature in every feature and look of the plain-spoken people who invited her, and it was not strange that she should feel an inclination to accept the invitation.   Her heart, weighed down with the sorrows of a life, and her mind, depressed with the gloom of unhappy forebodings, equally needed change; and as she sunk into the huge easy chair, she felt as if tears must betray either weakness or the susceptibility of her heart to the impression of kindness; indeed, it was the latter characteristic that caused the choking sensation which she felt, as an involuntary sigh escaped her lips.

As the hostess was pouring out the tea, Lizzy stole a glance at the well-folded and carefully sealed letter; she longed to press it to her lips, for it was written by the kindest of friends, and the mother of him who had made a world of sorrow beautiful and lovely, the sunlight of whose eyes had given hues to the flowers, and brightness even to the clouds, whose voice added sweetness to the nightingale's song, and music to the storms; whose love was to her as the sun to nature, in short, the heaven of her existence.

Evening soon began to fall, and the fading light warned Lizzie that it was time she returned to the Abbey. Her way was lonely, but there seemed little cause for apprehension, and she had not the least fear as she took her leave of the good-natured host and hostess.

As before stated, there was an immense lake-like sheet of water, in front of the "Talbot," stretching away to the right, over a broad expanse, and apparently losing itself amid the thick clusters of firs and beeches, with which it was partly surrounded. Either by mere chance, or from a motive of curiosity, the unsuspecting girl took the secluded path which wound round the silvery flood, instead of the more public and less attractive highway. It may have been from a desire to avoid the observation of any stray passenger or village gossip, who might by chance be coming to the inn, that she chose the green sward path.

The scene was particularly romantic and beautiful; the moon was just glancing with its full orb through the sable trees that formed the far background of the lake, while the calm surface of the water presented a pleasing contrast to the dark embankment of underwood with which the western side was shaded.

Charmed with the glowing scene, Lizzy tripped over the green sward with a light step, and a heart that seemed suddenly inspired with new hope; now thinking of the kindness of the good people of the inn, now of the inexpressible pleasure that awaited her in the letter, which she, ever and anon, pressed to her lips; now of her beloved Edgar, still beloved, though parted, maybe, for ever from her.

She was thus meditating, when suddenly from an obscure by-path, which otherwise would have eluded her observation, the figure of a man emerged and sauntered towards her. A single glance convinced her that it was Thornbury, but his purpose was by no means so apparent. A sudden pang darted through the girl's bosom, and a momentary pause ensued. She stood motionless for an instant; then looked round as if the thought of escaping her enemy by running back to the inn momentarily crossed her mind; but she was far—very far from the "Talbot." The path she had taken was exceedingly devious and intricate; but before she had time to decide, the voice of Thornbury, terrible and ominous, greeted her.

" Miss Wilmington," said he, " it's me."

Lizzy remained silent, the more so as the deep emphasis on the last word seemed to betoken the fiendish triumph of the adversary at finding her in a situation so much to his satisfaction.

" Why, ain't you afraid, Lizzy, with that pretty face o' yours, to be out at this 'ere lonely place at such a time. I wur afraid for yer, at any rate, for I knowed there was no grand young gentlemen hereabouts to take care of yer, and I wonder that one who sets such a high price upon 'erself don't take more care ; come on, my sweet bird, for I've come to see yer safe 'ome. I'm sure the old ooman will be fine and pleased at my taking care of yer ; why, I've been watchin' for yer for the last week, and you've kept your-self as close as a little mouse."

As the keeper spoke, he advanced towards the trembling girl, and it was apparent from his tone and manner that he was half-intoxicated; his demeanour, even for him, was unusually coarse and brutal, and the fiery glances of his cunning

eyes showed a fiendish determination that might
have struck terror into a bolder heart than that
of a defenceless girl in so lonely a situation.

Lizzy screamed, and the echo of her voice resounded through the forest of fir and brushwood
that stretched away to the eastern ridge of hills.

"That's no use now," said the dastardly
keeper; " there ain't no ear as can 'ear that, I'll
warrant thee, and d'ye mark it, it comes back
to us agin for want o' one ; devil's in the gal,
thee'l wake all the fes'nts in the persarves—'old
yer noise—d'ye think anybody wants to 'urt
yer ?"

"Let me alone," shrieked the girl, "I have
done you no harm ; why do you insult me ?"

"You're a lyin' jade," said Thornbury; " 'as
I ersulted thee ? if you say that agin I will call
you by another name than a wurchus gal, I warrant thee ; but come, I'll 'ave a taste o' your
lips, for wot gives pleasure to genlemen like
Hindly must be sweet."

"Go back!" exclaimed Lizzy; "keep off, I say."

The miserable girl shrieked and drew back, unconscious that she was so near the lake, which at this portion was unusually deep, and instead of becoming shallow as it approached the shore, washed against a precipitous bank—there Lizzy struggled as well as her feeble strength would admit; and, as she buffetted her adversary with her arms, excited him the more; his fiendish nature was mad with passion, and the thought of dashing her headlong into the flood below darted across his mind. He was in a fit of demoniacal rage, and in another instant his murderous intention would have been carried into execution; at this moment, however, the sound of oars caught his ear, and, murderer as he had resolved to be, he was not so mad as to carry out his devilish purpose in the face of witnesses. Seizing his almost helpless burden by the waist, he partly lifted her from the ground and dragged her, screaming, from the position of danger in which she was placed.

" Fool !" he exclaimed, " I 'ave at least saved yer life; if it 'ad'nt a bin for me you'd ha' bin in that there pond, and I'll warrant yer yer might 'ave roared long enough for help there."

" Let me go, in Heaven's name. Spare me! spare me! Oh, for the sake of my mother, spare me. Why—why would you harm me?"

" 'Arm the devil, gal, who wants to 'arm yer; you'll make me mad presently, with that d——d forlse tongue; but come, I don't want to carry yer if yer'll walk. 'Ave I cut yer legs off, or what the devil ails yer?"

" Let me go," exclaimed Lizzy, making another effort to escape his grasp.

" I ain't the fool you take me for," said Thornbury, clutching her more tightly, and endeavouring to pollute her cheeks with kisses. " By G—d," he exclaimed, " you're a tough pullet, too, and a wild un, but you'll be tamed."

By this time the villain had hurried his victim into a dense part of the copse or thicket, some distance from the pond, and was still urging her forward, albeit her limbs were scarcely able to sustain their weight. Her resistance every instant goaded her adversary, and inflamed more and more his violent nature, till at last, roused to his utmost fury, he determined upon revenge or victory.

"Look, 'ere" he exclaimed, " we are orffered five 'underd pounds. Will you rob me of my charnce ?"

" No, no; not rob you," said Lizzy.

" Then you'll be mine from this 'ere moment, this wery minut."

Lizzy's tears burst forth as though her heart had dissolved, and her violent emotions seemed to render her utterly helpless. In another instant she rallied; more than her usual strength returned, and she seemed determined to struggle to the death with her enemy. But Thornbury, tall and powerful, caught her by the waist, and with apparently little effort, lifted her from the ground, and then dashed her upon it with a bitter oath.

At this instant a sudden blow from the cudgel of a tall gipsy-looking man, felled the villain to the earth, where he lay motionless, and like one dead—a heavy groan, the grating of teeth, and a half-uttered curse, however, gave sufficient evidence that the wretch was yet alive.

Lizzy had recovered herself sufficiently to rise, and as she staggered towards a tree, the athletic arm of her stalwart deliverer gently supported her, as gently as if she had been an infant in its first attempt to stand alone.

" Lady," said the gipsy, " where do yer want to go?   I'll see yer safe, lady."

" My good friend," exclaimed Lizzy, " how can I thank you?"

" Never mind thankin' me, never mind that," said the gipsy, " but whither away is the home ye'd be at?   Nay, ye mun lean on this arm, and here's the other that'll fight for yer, as if ye was taking me straight away to Heaven, and the devil would stand atween us."

Lizzy was scarcely able to listen or reply, for the sense of danger that had hitherto imparted unusual energy, now that it was subsiding, awakened a keen perception of the awful position from which she had been rescued, and proportionately diminished her strength. The gipsy, however, bravely supported her, and bore her gently forward, watching her face as her head rested upon his shoulder with the most tender solicitude. It was evident that she was growing weaker; and, as her pale features received the light of the moon through an opening in the thicket, they seemed almost too beautiful to be human.

"My poor bairn," said the gipsy, "cheer up, you're safe now, chiel, and shall soon be away to the house yon, for I see ye're from Heathmoor; and by the love of Heaven we've heard o' thy kindness to our tribe. Cheer up, lady, here's a spring."

As he spoke he stooped with his lovely burden, and taking some of the clear cool water that gurgled from the root of an ancient oak, bathed her forehead with it. The effect was almost instantaneous; a heavy sigh escaped her lips, and her eyes were fixed upon the face of her deliverer.

" Bee'st better, lady ?"

" Where—who—where am I?" asked the girl.

" Safe, safe, anyhow," said the gipsy, " and 'll be at Heathmoor soon."

"Yes, yes," said Lizzy, " Heathmoor! that is it; but who—who are you?"

" I'm but a rough un to handle such as you," said the gipsy, "but I'll handle yer smoothly, anyhow. Can yer walk a little, my maid ?"

" Yes, yes," said Lizzy, leaning upon the arm that supported her. " Oh, how can I thank you for this ?"

" You're from Heathmoor," said the gipsy, "and must be the lady whose goodness made our tribe bless yer. It's strange if I mightn't do yer a good turn without any thankin' for it; but who was that there feller?"

Lizzy's breath checked her as she was about to utter the name; and she paused till the gipsy repeated his enquiry.

" I must not tell," said she, " for it would be dangerous to mention even—"

" Dangerous!" remarked the gipsy, with some surprise, " he must be a markable man if he gets over the blow I gave un. He must be drove out o' the country."

" Nay," said Lizzy, " but, for the present at least, I would not let this matter be known."

" You knows him," said the gipsy. " He looked summut like a keeper."

" Yes," said Lizzy, " he is a keeper at Heath-moor."

" The same chap as set the dog at Tim and me," muttered the gipsy; and his teeth clenched and grated as the circumstance came to his mind.

" You have repaid him for it," said Lizzy, fearing that the revenge should be even yet more complete.

"I've only 'alf paid un yet what we owes un, and if I'd know'd—"

"Stay," said Lizzy, "you must not, for my sake, do him any further harm. You will not? promise me that."

"A ——— willain," remarked the gipsy, rather to himself than Lizzy, "he ain't fit to live, he ain't."

By this time they had reached the highroad, for, well acquainted with every track and byway of that wild region, the gipsy had conducted his fair charge by the nearest route. Once more Lizzy was in sight of her temporary home, and would willingly have dismissed her deliverer with a repetition of her thanks, but she feared lest further vengeance might be taken on her enemy. She grasped the hand of her protector, and begged earnestly that he would desist from further injuring him.

"I'll see whether un be dead or alive though," answered the gipsy.

"But for my sake don't hurt him."

"He's weak now, I'll warrant thee, queen; and I won't take the benefit of ur's weakness; but I might meet un agin, and then I'll settle scores wi' un."

"I have a little money," said Lizzy, "and though it will be no reward for such services, it will be a more substantial token of my gratitude than all my thanks."

"Nay," said the gipsy, "we be beggars when need be, but we never earns money by doin' a bit o' kindness. We knows what we be, but there's some natur' in us arter all; and I'd as lif think o' taking them bright eyes from yer as money for what I've done: your kind face is pay enough. God bless yer sweet face, and send a blessed sweetheart for't. Nay, I wun't ha' them tears, nuther, for I ain't desarved 'em. Please Heaven, though, I may see yer face when a brighter sun shines on it than seems to ha' done o' late—for Dorcas told us—"

"What do you mean?" asked Lizzy, amazed at the quickness of the gipsy's discernment.

" Mean ?" he replied; " yer remembers the lanky, dark-haired gal of our tribe that met yer on the brow o' Lammas hill one arternoon at sunset ?"

" Yes, yes !" replied Lizzy, " but her tale, though well told, and I might wish would turn out true, yet never, never can be. My lot has been sad, and must remain sad; but does she relate round your camp fire the tales she tells others about their fortunes ?"

" I can make out your meaning, lady, though your words be a bit too high. But Dorcas told us your tale, and will tell it for many a night to come, I warrant thee."

" Nay," said Lizzy, rather to herself than her protector, " I must escape—I must go away from Heathmoor. Oh, Heaven, what will become of me ?" and as she spoke the tears gushed from her eyes, and she sobbed with that violence which sometimes precedes hysterical grief.

" The Lord will take cake o' thee, child," said

the gipsy. "Come, you morn't take on so; cheer up, lass, here's the road to the little gate in the wall."

"Bless you for your kindness," said Lizzy. "Good-bye; there's my mother watching for me at the gate."

Lizzy was in tears as she fell upon her mother's neck, and for some moments could scarcely utter a syllable. She walked to the house with her arm clutching that of her mother. It was some time before she could relate the dreadful circumstances that had attended her journey, and, for awhile she forgot even the letter which had been the object of her visit to the inn. As she became more composed, however, she remembered it, and searched for it, but it was gone. In vain she taxed her memory as to when she saw it last. The circumstances of her unhappy journey seemed like a dream. Her brain grew dizzy, her sight failed, and visions of unutterable horror appalled her imagination till she sank into a state of unconsciousness. The shock had been too much for her nervous system. Thus she remained for some hours.

The gipsy, meanwhile, had retraced his steps through that wild region which he had so lately traversed; his bold heart, unconscious of fear, exulted in the good fortune which had thrown him in the way of one whom he regarded as an enemy, at such a juncture. Almost noiselessly, and with the stealthy tread of a cat seeking its prey, he threaded the intricate byways of the wood, prepared for an onslaught, should his adversary attack him; but at the same time apprehensive that he might find him as he had left him, rather than in a position to afford a second opportunity of treating the keeper to a " thwack of his trusty thorn." As he approached the spot where he expected to find Thornbury lying, he slackened his pace and listened, but there was no sound save the murmur of the wind. Without further hesitation, therefore, he advanced, and as

he broke through the brushwood in a different
course to that by which he had left the scene of the
recent conflict, he found that Thornbury was gone.
There were blood stains upon the grass where he
had lain, which showed that the villain had bled
profusely.

"That's well, that's well," murmured the gipsy,
"I be glad I ain't killed yer, I be glad; the
marks o' thy blood be better on the grass than
on my hands; but I a'most killed thee, and that
makes me glad too.   It must ha' been a blow to
knock down a bullock wi', and thy head maun be
as thick as a skittle pin not to gone to pieces.
They says we ain't honest, but the deil's in't if
we ever pay sic debts wi' poundage.   Here be
news for Sim and Tim and Billy.   Now for the
camp, but stay—"

Thus muttering to himself, the gipsy pursued
his journey through the densest of the thicket in
search of his nocturnal sport, and then worked
his way unmolested to the encampment, which

was situated not far from Heathmoor, but in a different direction to that in which it was when Edgar Hindly, some months after, accidentally made the acquaintance of the same gipsy.

CHAPTER X.

THE CAUSE OF MRS. HINDLY'S DEATH.

To a person of such keen sensibility as the gallant Thornbury, the reflections and apprehensions which occupied his mind, as he awoke from the stupor into which the stunning blow had involved him, were by no means of a pleasant nature. As he first opened his eyes upon the flood of moonlight there was an utter forgetfulness of all that had taken place. Why he should be lying where he was in such a state of prostrate helplessness, he was unable to conceive; but a sharp, smarting pain on the left side of his head, as though he had been bitten by an adder, recalled to his mind the figure of Lizzy Wilmington, his awkward attempt to insult her, and the sudden and uncomfortable sensation of a huge cudgel coming into collision with his ill-fated skull; but from what hand the blow had come he was in no wise capable of conceiving, the administration of it having been alike unexpected and invisible. So Thornbury lay like one who suddenly awakes from a horrible dream, staring at vacancy, and half wondering whether he was recollecting what had actually taken place, or was recalling a vision.

Suddenly, he grated his teeth, and bit his lips, swore, and attempted to rise ; but as he regained his feet, his legs trembled, his brain grew dizzy, his body reeled, and he fell.

Who could have thought it? That huge, strong, domineering villain, who but lately was lording it over an unprotected girl, and tossing her up and down as though she had been a toy in his power-

ful grasp, now unable to support his own weight.
A single blow from a stout cudgel has made him
such that a child might punish him as it pleased!

He kept on cursing the pain, and then the
hand that had inflicted it. The blood was still
flowing, and when he discovered it, a sickening,
fainting sensation overpowered him. Tearing his
handkerchief from his neck, he bound up the
wound as well as he could, and in a few minutes,
attempted once more to walk. He was this time
more successful, but was so weak that he leant
for support against a tree. As he stood tottering,
his eye caught sight of the letter which Lizzy had
looked upon, and cherished with so much delight;
he picked it up, and thrusting it into his pocket,
withdrew from the spot where he had fallen, and
crawling into the densest copse he could find,
again laid himself upon the ground. Here he
must have been when the gipsy passed on his
journey to the camp, for the first rays of the sun
were tinging the horizon before he awoke from
the sound sleep into which he had fallen.

In Thornbury there was nothing of shame; fear, there was much; and as he reflected on the work of the past night he cursed the girl he had sought to injure; and with a bitter oath determined to take vengeance upon her as the cause of his calamity. But as yet he dared not appear at Heathmoor, for he feared lest the actions which looked innocent enough to him might be called crimes by others. He felt that he had a powerful supporter in Walters, but yet there was someone who had been a witness of his outrage upon the girl; and, even if he had to encounter the anger of the rustics it was more than he could comfortably endure; apart from the apprehension of his being taken prisoner, and tried for—he didn't quite know what. So he prudently resolved to watch the movements of " the wench;" and, at the same time, conceal himself from observation for the present.

Lizzy was still a sufferer from the severe shock her nervous system had sustained, and for some days was confined to her chamber; so great, however, was her dread of Thornbury, that she resolved to quit Heathmoor as soon as her strength would permit. The grief, at the loss of the letter, was poignant in the extreme, and the apprehension that it had fallen into the hands of her enemy was an additional cause of vexation, for her beloved benefactress had enjoined the strictest secresy concerning it. On the sixth morning after the almost fatal occurrence, she was sufficiently restored in health to contemplate her departure, but whither she should direct her steps was a question not easily solved; and the idea of separating from her mother was no less a source of sorrow or difficulty.

"I think," said Mrs. Wilmington, "we had better remain a little time, the villain will not venture here again. He has not been heard of since."

"Nay, mother," answered Lizzy, "but his defeat will incite him the more to the revenge which he contemplates. No, let me go at all events; I would sooner seek a home in the gipsy encampment, where I am sure of protection, than remain here, where I know my life is in danger. He is not far away, depend on it."

"God has protected you most mercifully, my child," said Mrs. Wilmington, "and He will yet befriend us."

"But I cannot remain," said Lizzy, "you do not know his savage nature. That horrid look— I cannot—I never shall forget it."

Their deliberations were abruptly ended by the appearance of a horseman riding up the avenue. His nearer approach showed him to be no other than Mr. Hindly. Dismounting from his horse, which he gave into the keeping of the gardener, he entered the house, and in a little while was heard calling loudly for Wilmington.

"He is mad," said Lizzy, "do not answer him, he has no power over us here."

"Wilmington!" again shouted the Squire, as his heavy step was heard approaching the chamber.

Lizzy was somewhat excited, and her complexion grew pale as she heard him lift the latch. Her mother sat composed and calm, waiting his entrance.

"Wilmington!" said he, as he entered, "I command you instantly to leave this place; and you too (turning to Lizzy), disgrace of your sex, be off with you."

"We did not come here by your authority," said Mrs. Wilmington, "and we shall not leave by your commands."

"Infamous creature!" said Hindly, "bandy no words with me, but be off."

"It is time," said Lizzy, "when murderers track us. Come, mother, let us go."

Hindly turned from them in rage, and walked to and fro the apartment as if waiting immediate obedience to his orders.

There was a smile of contempt on the lips of the old lady as she rose to pack up her scanty wardrobe; and, as she looked into the face of Hindly, there seemed in her glance more of defiance than submission.

" Mr. Hindly," she said.

" Silence!" said the Squire, " I will hear nothing from you."

" But you shall hear me ask the reason of this new charge against the character of my daughter," said Mrs. Wilmington.

" Go!" exclaimed Hindly.

" Yes; and I go," answered the old lady, " to protest against this murderous attempt on my daughter's life; there is something in it which shows that the wretch who attacked her was acting as the instrument of a greater villain, if that can be, than himself."

" Who?—what do you mean?"

" Time will tell you both," replied Mrs. Wilmington; " but thus far I will explain—my daughter's life has been attempted by the fellow who followed us hither, at someone's bidding; it may have been yours, or it must have been at that of Sir Robert Walters, with whom I have something to transact when the time comes."

" You rave, woman."

" Yes ; and there are others who will rave, too, when they hear me talk. Mark me, Mr. Hindly, this deed shall not go unpunished; and those who sought the life of my innocent girl shall bitterly rue it. There's a murderer among you."

" I will have you punished if you talk like that," said Hindly.

" You dare not face me in a court of justice," said Mrs. Wilmington, " neither you nor Walters. Look you, Mr. Hindly, I charge you both with cowardice, and one of you with a murderous assault upon my poor girl. Make me prove it— make me prove it—and punish me if you dare."

" Hag !" exclaimed Hindly, fiercely, and with a countenance pale with rage; " you are drunk, and it was only the other night your daughter was found on the common on her return from the inn. Thornbury came to her assistance, and the reward was a villainous attack from the hand of her paramour—my son; and the letter, which was dropped by the intoxicated girl was a communication from my wife. Base woman, you

have inveigled my son into this disgraceful connection, and by your cursed witchcraft have imposed upon my credulous wife; but I will have
you for this charge against Sir Robert."

Mrs. Wilmington's emotions at the unjust
accusation against her daughter seemed to prevent
her utterance. She paused for some moments,
watching the countenance of Hindly, as though
she were weighing every thought that passed
through his mind; and then said—"The fear of
the murderer drives us, not your command.
Again, Mr. Hindly, I say it, a murderer has been
sent upon our track, and five hundred pounds is
the price of my daughter's blood—do you hear
it? Ha! ha! you sent a poor woman to jail for
less than that—less than that, Mr. Hindly; but
here is one whom neither you nor the baronet
that lives near you will venture to punish. But
you may take this to the good Sir Robert, if you
will, that there is a story of the Peninsula that is
not to be found in books—a romantic story—and
one of India—India, Squire Hindly; but enough,

those who keep murderers must have long purses."

The manner and tone of Mrs. Wilmington as she spoke these words were well calculated to impress Hindly with the idea that she was under some extraordinary delusion. Her whole visage assumed an appearance of terrible excitement; and it seemed, as if involuntarily, she uttered language, the import of which was mysterious, even as the words seemed incoherent.

Hindly gave one look, then turned away, and hastily quitted the apartment, fully impressed with the idea that she was rather an object of pity than punishment; that she was in fact, mad. He beckoned Lizzy to follow.

" Not a step," said her mother ; " here in my presence speak, if you have anything to say. I know your thoughts, sir ; you believe I am deranged. Heaven knows I have suffered enough to derange me, but my memory is good."

" Mother, let me go," said Lizzy, " this is useless. Mr. Hindly, I have nothing to ask you to forgive, but I pray Heaven to be more merciful to you than you have been to my poor mother. Your charges against me are false and cowardly, and what my mother has affirmed with regard to the keeper is as true as that Heaven was the witness of it all. He was sent to murder me; and this will I charge him with in any court of justice that you dare bring the matter into—whether you or Sir Robert sent him is a matter which you can decide between you; but you have within you a safe and sure witness that will not lie, and cannot forget."

" This shall be seen into," said Hindly.

Thus saying, he left the house, mounted his horse, and rode away. His mind was harassed with a thousand thoughts, and it seemed as if a sudden dread had seized him, and if Mrs. Wilmington had possessed the powers of witchcraft which he attributed to her, she could scarcely have employed them more efficaciously in working a change upon an enemy than was apparent in the proud and haughty Squire of Raymonds. The last rebuke of Lizzy seemed more severe than that of her mother, for with her there had been a calmness of tone and manner that rebutted any suspicion of her being under the same influence, whether of madness or witchcraft, as her parent. Hindly returned to Raymonds, and at once proceeded to question his wife respecting the persons whom he had visited at Heathmoor.

Mrs. Hindly was at a loss to conjecture the reason of his absence, for since he left Raymonds on the morning when he met Sir Robert and Lady Walters in the park he had not returned. The letter which was lying at Burwell revealed a circumstance which was alike inexplicable to himself and the Walters family ; the nature of which it may be convenient to lay before the reader.

It was in the handwriting of Thornbury, and ran as follows :—

" HONORED SIR,—

"The inside is wot I found yistrday, bein' droppd from yung Wilmington, who wor a comin' from the publikouse, drurnk, which she has bin in the abbit of goin' to evry day. She are queare as ever she wor, and I thinks is married to our young maister. Her mither ur a reglar witch, as is thort by evry boddy heare."

The letter referred to was eagerly opened by Sir Robert, although it bore marks of having been subjected to a like operation by a hand that had clumsily re-sealed it. It was, as already stated, from Mrs. Hindly, and was worded as follows :—

"MY DEAR MRS. WILMINGTON,—

"Thornbury has left Burwell; for what purpose I cannot conjecture. Let me advise you to beware of him, for I feel convinced that he is an evilly-disposed fellow. If you can, I would recommend you to leave Heathmoor without delay; but why not at once assert your right, and demand reparation. However, I will keep the secret, although I shall use every means to ascertain the information you require. But leave Heathmoor, and let me know where you are. Give my

love to dear Lizzy, and tell her that I shall ever
regard her as my own daughter, and shall be
proud to acknowledge her."

What were the feelings of Sir Robert and Lady
Walters, or of Squire Hindly it is impossible to
say.   Everyone was pale with emotion, and presented an aspect such as those only manifest who
plot deeply, and are suddenly surprised by de-
tection.

Lady Walters was the first to speak, and she
began to comment upon the matter by vituperat-
ing Mrs. Hindly, as acting a part against the
interest of her husband, of herself, and of everybody else.   Hindly said nothing, but hastily
quitted the house, and proceeded to Heathmoor.
On his return he found his wife low-spirited and
dejected.   Her delicate health was no shield
against the rage of her husband, who burst into
the chamber with a bitter exclamation, such as
had never escaped his lips since the day that Mrs.
Hindly first knew him.

" Traitress !" said he, " you are no longer worthy to be called my wife; and—what is this you
have done? Acknowledge that girl as your
daughter! You are base, worthless, and odious
in my sight."

" What is it?" asked Mrs. Hindly.

" Will you?—nay, Amelia—we are divorced—
I have read your treachery in your own handwriting. You have assented to a marriage, alike
dishonourable and—and—we are ruined; and the
sooner we separate the better for our peace. My
home and yours must henceforth be different.
My G—d, could I have expected this from you!"

Hindly paused from the violence of his rage.
Words forced themselves to his lips too fast for
utterance; and his sentences seemed to resolve
themselves into foam; his eyes glared like those
of a madman; his massive frame tottered with
anger; and, as he flung himself into a chair, it
seemed as if his face would burst into flame.

Mrs. Hindly felt as if she had been guilty of a
crime; and she struggled between the duty of

confessing the secret of Mrs. Wilmington, and the obligation of a promise which she held sacred.

"Have patience," said she, "and you shall be satisfied. I have done wrong to a certain extent, but if wrong was ever excusable, I have an excuse. Nay, my husband, I have not willingly nor wilfully deceived you. I have been no party to the matter of Edgar and Lizzy; but there is yet something to be told respecting her that will alter your opinion, both with regard to her and me."

"Attempt no excuse," said Hindly, "for there is none; none! by Heaven—none. You have been imposed upon by a base wretch who is unworthy the name of woman; and you have betrayed me. Your letter is in the hands of Walters—your own words. Your letter, I say, is with Walters; the girl was drunk, and dropped it; Thornbury found it, and sent it to his master. The clearest evidence in the world. It only remains for him to sell us out, and then our ways separate."

"Nay," said Mrs. Hindly, imploring, and with evidently some effort to soothe her enraged husband; "he will not—he cannot—"

"Will not; what the devil do you mean? I tell you that this headstrong folly of yours has already ruined us; and now, you say, it cannot be—it is so, you fool. Heaven's curse upon you —you—you have done it all. You've ruined me, I tell you—ruined me—d—— you. Go, I'll never see you again."

Mrs. Hindly rose hastily from her seat to check her husband, and she nearly succeeded in throwing her arms around him as he quitted the apartment and reached the landing of the grand staircase; but he thrust her from him violently; she staggered several steps, and then fell; her strength was not sufficient to enable her to recover her balance, and she was precipitated to the bottom of the stairs, where she lay, for awhile, in a state of unconsciousness. There was no one near to witness the unhappy circumstance; and Hindly descended hastily, and with a feeling of inexpressible horror, lifted the almost breathless body of his wife. She was as pale as death, and her head fell back over her husband's arm.

At this juncture, the reader will trace in his mind the course of events to the moment Edgar was summoned to his mother's bedside. Her generous and gentle nature had not suffered her to breathe a word of the cause of the fatal occurrence; and she endeavoured to persuade herself that it was the result of her weakness rather than the angry act of her husband.

Hindly was not without some of the better feelings of humanity; and, for awhile, the cause of his anger was merged in the consequence. Bitter tears were shed as he leaned over the dying form of his suffering wife. Remembrances of other days *would* crowd upon his mind, and the harsh, unfeeling language he had used to her aggravated his sorrow. But all was too late for reparation; and though he could forgive the vague tale which his wife told him upon her deathbed respecting Wilmington, yet he had a thought that his wife's romantic disposition had betrayed her into an error, which resulted in the ruin of himself, and the disgrace of every member of the family.

CHAPTER XI.

" STILL ACHIEVING."

Job's success was almost equal to the patience of his patriarchal namesake; and it is hardly necessary to say that the elder Hawkins was delighted with the increased rents which poured into his strong box, and thence into his banker's, under his son's careful superintendence. Indeed, so great had his confidence in " the boy " become, that the whole of his affairs (with the exception of making his will) were left entirely to his management. The old man had grown too feeble

for exertion, but he composed himself very comfortably in his easy chair, drank his rum and
water, and chuckled over his growing fortune.
From time to time, as the money in the strong box
increased, Job was commissioned to invest it at the
banker's—a task always acceptable to the boy,
and performed with a correctness, which did him
much credit. Each time the banker's book was
produced it was accurate to a shilling, and as the
old man carefully closed the clasp, and deposited
the little volume in his desk, he would utter his
favourite words—" wast always a good boy, Job ;
wast always a good boy." In the father's eyes
Job was a prodigy ; a rising, clever lad who
would one day achieve great things. He was
already a man of fashion, and the pet of many a
gay circle. Known to the world as a liberal supporter of almost every charitable institution in
London, a subscriber to the hospitals, a patron of
art and science, and an advocate for the diffusion
of useful knowledge. His name figured con-
spicuously in many a committee ; and, as fame

reported him the son of a millionaire, the world hoped great things from him, while many a marriageable damsel and ambitious mother regarded him with aspirations, such as only mothers with such daughters, and daughters with such desires can indulge.

But Job was in a higher region than any of these untitled dames or damsels; like Jack on his beanstalk he had attained to such a height of glory and grandeur that he might well wonder in what sublime sphere his future destiny might be fixed. Numerous invitations had been received by him to "stand" for boroughs; and it was hardly to be supposed that a man of such transcendant qualities could long resist the temptation to enter upon the new field which the senate chamber opened to him. To benefit the human race was his mission, and to sweep away the abuses of our constitution should henceforth be his object. He never entertained a doubt of his ability to accomplish either, for his friends unhesitatingly pronounced him the cleverest man of

the day. A man who possessed his affable manner, who moved in such good circles, and lived
in Mayfair, must be somebody to envy and
admire. He said funny things too, and always
produced the very prettiest laughs and giggles
from the admiring fair. The result of all was
that he condescended to be returned at the head
of the poll for the borough of ——. His speech
at the Town Hall was received with exclamations
of applause, such as never greet anyone but a
really great man. His sentences were constantly
interrupted with unanimous cries of " hear, hear ;"
and it was evident to all his constituents that the
great man was come who was to accomplish the
reconstruction of the British constitution, to place
the throne on a firmer basis, to tear down the
partition wall between classes, and to elevate the
very meanest costermonger to the level of the
nobleman. "The people's rights" was his text;
and, as he promised to alter everything according
to everybody's taste, everybody was pleased. So
great, indeed, had he become as the champion of

the people's liberties, that even Friday, as he walked behind him, was cheered by the people almost as much as his master. Friday was a great man, too.

Nor was all this very wonderful to those who had made society their study.

The many thousands who gazed on the "mountain of light," at the Exhibition of eighteen hundred and fifty one, with the exception of a few individuals, perhaps, would have lavished upon it the same applause had a piece of glass been substituted for the real "Koh-i-noor." Nor is this to pronounce men fools; it is simply to assert that the intrinsic worth of an object is less frequently the subject of public applause than the rumoured estimate of it. Imagination is greater than fact.

But Job was not of a proud disposition by any means. It was wonderful with what affability and unreserved familiarity he came down from the House of Commons, and took his seat in the dirty office of the Hebrew money-lender. After listening to discussions involving the fate of empires he would converse in the most frank and easy manner about bills and bonds, mortgages and notes.

One night, after a very important debate, the hon. gentleman descended from the summit of his beanstalk, and found himself in company with Solomon.

" Well, Sol," he said, " what news?—anything of your friend, yet?—paid you?"

" Mein Got, nay; but shtay, Mr Hawkinsh, shtay; I have a packet which cosht me mush monish; shome deedsh, I bleeve, but they are in de foreign English."

" Foreign English, eh," said Job.

" Ay, de flourishing—"

" I understand you; let me see them."

" Nay," said the Jew, " but dey are a shecret; and, I bleeve, conshernsh thish shame Mashter Hindly."

" Let me have them," said Job, " I will soon tell you if they are worth anything."

"Wort anyting; why, de devil! didn't I tell you dey cosht me mush monish."

"That doesn't alter their value, my friend. How did you get them?"

"How!" exclaimed Solomon, "why by honesht meansh to be shure, ash I do alwaysh get everyting honesht, don't I?"

"Of course," replied Job, "honesty, you know, will carry a man through the world as fast as a horse can gallop."

"To be shure it will, Mr. Hawkinsh, to be shure it will; and de oder ting ish ash likely to break a man'sh neck ash look at him. Now deshe papersh, you shee—"

"But I don't see them yet," said the advocate of the honest policy.

"No, but you shall shee 'em, after I tell you where dey come from."

"So long as they didn't come from the devil," said Job, "I don't care, but I want no deed of his."

"De devil!" said Solomon, "why you shay dat?

Money ish money, my good share; and if it bear de king'sh head, a lawful stamp head, I don't care if it come from de devil'sh hand, mind me, Mr. Hawkinsh, if it'sh honesht come by. De man may be a tief dat bring it. No matter, it ish de hand dat takesh, not givesh, dat make it good deed or bad."

"But you got this wonderful packet somewhere, and somehow?" remarked Job.

"Coursh I did, share; it wash at de butter shop, and I bought it for mush monish, for de name, I tought, might probable be shomething to go by. Now dish ish de ting."

Thus saying, he took from his pocket a lot of loose parchment engrossed in the manner of ancient deeds; and, submitting them, one at a time, to the perusal of Job, watched his countenance, meanwhile, with the most scrutinizing glance, in order to detect, by the expression, whether his bargain was likely to be advantageous or not.

"These are nothing," said Job, carelessly flinging the last sheet across the table.

"Notting!" exclaimed the Jew. "Now, by Got, I would contradict you, but you are a shentleman, and in Parliament, and have promised to get de Jewsh dere."

"And will perform it," said Job, smiling; "but these deeds seem worthless. If you like to let me peruse them at my leisure I will give you my opinion."

The old man carefully folded the dirty parchments, and tied them with the string, on which was a broken seal.

"If dey are wort notting I will loseh my bargain, dat ish all," said the Jew, "but I tink I read your eye, Mr. Hawkinsh, while you read de papersh."

"You're a keen rogue," said Job. "What did you read?"

"Read!" said the Jew; "I have not lived shixty-five year, and not learn dat de look contradict de tongue shometimsh. Now it shtrike me deshe papersh are shometing to do wid de eshtate dat you want to mortgage. I not part wid de papersh, dey cosht me mush monish."

"I don't want them," said Job; "they are deeds as you know, and they may relate to Heathmoor; but I should advise you to have a care as to the account you give of the manner by which you came by them. Butter shops are not usually the places in which we discover family writings."

"What!" said Solomon, with a peculiar twinkle of the eye; "you tink I lie, Mashter Hawkinsh. I shwear it ish true, true as shunrishe."

"I don't doubt your word," answered Job; "but I feel bound to tell you that there has been a burglary committed at this same Heathmoor."

"Burglare—burglare—what ish de burglare to do wid deshe? When wash de burglare?"

"The night before last," said Job, "and several pieces of plate have been stolen, together with a packet of writings."

The countenance of Solomon changed at this intelligence.

"I don't want to alarm you," continued Job, "but advise you to deliver them up as soon as possible. Honesty, you know, is the best policy."

"Honeshty!" said Solomon—"it ish my macshim—de besht polishy ish de besht polishy; but I get dem for mush monish, and I will have my monish before I give dem up. But de devil! a burglare at Heatmoor. I know notting of de burglare."

"It may be," said Job, "and I should be sorry to think you knew anything more of it than I; but if Mr. Hindly should find them in your possession?"

"He shall have dem for de monish I give, but not one farden lesh."

"But that is hardly the point," said Job. "These parchments may be the deeds relating to the title—I say they *may* be; and if so—"

"And if sho," answered Solomon, "dey are de more valuable—more valuable."

"But you dare not retain them."

"I dare put dem on de firesh," answered the Jew, angrily.

"It is nothing to me," said Job; "but if you wish to hold them safely I will give you a bit of advice; but perhaps—"

"Yesh, yesh; I will lishen, Mashter Hawkinsh, to de bit of advish."

"You must advance money upon them," said Job.

"Advansh! why you alwaysh shay advansh! Why, ish not Hindly in my debt already, and I buy deshe writingsh? Bah! I won't advansh upon my own propertish."

"Very well," said Job; "as I said before I have no interest in the matter, but as a friend I tell you it is not safe to keep them."

"Den you betray me! do you?"

"Not I," said Job; "but do you not see that if you hold them as security by way of equitable mortgage you will have evidence of the manner by which you became possessed of them. You needn't advance much; but you are in positive peril, the peril at least of having to give the most straightforward account of the persons from whom you took them. A letter from Mr. Hindly would do it all."

"Whew!" said the Jew; "I she, I she; and den de eshtate will be mortgage to me. I will shee. Mortgage, yesh."

"I have no objection," said Job, "to draw up a document between you and Mr. Hindly, and doing the whole thing for you; but it's a dangerous business."

The old man seemed to think there was some truth in Job's remarks, and a great deal of sense in his reasoning.

"Look," said Job, "if Hindly knew you had them he would certainly demand an explanation; now, I can effect the matter even without letting him know that you are in possession of deeds that may, by some contingency, one day be of importance; and, indeed, which—"

"But he musht shign de paper," said Solomon.

"I will manage to obtain his signature if you advance sufficient," said Job. "A needy man, you know, who deals in bills and post-obits, is seldom very inquisitive as to the nature of the instrument he signs, if by signing he obtains a handsome sum. You will be safe; but I would advise you to act without delay. This robbery has made a stir, and the papers say they have a clue to the perpetrators of it."

Solomon loved his money; and although, to a great extent, it made him forget the danger, whenever an opportunity of gain was before him, yet there were times when a footstep on the pavement caused him to listen with an indescribable feeling of apprehension. In the present instance he felt far more awkwardly situated with regard to the papers than he cared to discover to his friend. He did not, therefore, adopt too eagerly the plan suggested, for fear of awakening a suspicion in the mind of Hawkins. Nevertheless, he resolved to leave the matter in his hands; and, relying upon his own cunning, thought the advantage would ultimately result to himself. The conclusion, therefore, of the discussion was, that Job was to transact the matter between Mr. Hindly and Solomon; a business which the hon. gentleman was well qualified to perform without the intervention of the Squire.

Job, therefore, prepared a document, purporting to deposit with Solomon certain deeds and do-cuments relating to the estate of Heathmoor, by way of security for certain sums already advanced, with interest thereon; and uncertain other sums to be advanced, from time to time, as the said Edgar Hindly should require. With this simple document carefully folded, on the following night the indefatigable Job presented himself at the office of the usurer, or as he was described in the instrument, " merchant."

" Why," said the Jew, " pon my shoul, share, you have no done de businessh already !"

" Here is the instrument," said Job, " signed and witnessed, sealed and delivered. I thought a deed would be preferable, under the circumstances, to a mere acknowledgment."

"Zactly," said Solomon. "Now let me shee vot you shay, share—vot you shay?" As he spoke he took the instrument in his hand, and looked carefully at the signature. "But how de devil! Ish Mashter Hindly in town, share?"

"I have been down to him," answered the lawyer.

"Oh, ah, I shee—I shee. And who ish dish shentleman'sh shignature—de witnessh here—Fri—Fri—Frid—ish it Friday? Dat ish a weekday name."

"It's my clerk's," said Job. "The other is the Reverend Charles Mackenzie."

"Dat vill do. Now let me read. You have made me shecure for de monish advanshed?"

"Here you see," answered Job, pointing to the "recital," and hurrying his friend along at a pace which tended more to the confusion than the elucidation of the matter—"You see I had two or three different obstacles to encounter; two or three difficult matters to arrange for your perfect security, and—"

"Why, what ish dish?" exclaimed Solomon; "by Eliash and all de prophetsh, I—what—five hundred poundsh; I will not advansh but fifty on it, and dat ish forty-nine too mush."

"Well," said Job, "I am only the attorney for you. Give me back the deed, and my business is at an end, so far as I am concerned. I only wish that I knew nothing of the matter, except that, for your sake, I wish you had never seen those d—— parchments.

The old man looked up, and darted a glance in which anger and fear mingled—a glance, however, sufficiently expressive for Job who felt his power over the stubborn money-lender.

"Do as you will," said he; "but let me tell you what, perhaps, is no news to you, that those papers have been stolen with other things from Heathmoor within the last few days. So far from their being valuable to you, however, they may cost you your life. Nay, don't start, my friend, for it's not certain yet whether the thief is apprehended; but even if he never should be, how will you venture to avail yourself of this bargain?"

"What bargain?" demanded Solomon.

"With the mysterious butterman."

"Den I burn deshe parchment," said the Jew.

"Very well, get out of your danger as you think best."

"And if I give five hundred pound for dem I am shafe, eh? Mr. Hawkinsh, dat ish pretty law; de lawsh are not made for honesht men."

"This is what will make you safe," answered Job, pointing at the same time to the signature of Edgar Hindly.

"And how will dat make me shafe?"

"Is it not evidence of the best kind that you came by those deeds honestly, my friend; who is to dispute a fact so apparent? Why, if you had stolen them yourself this would screen you from the charge."

The old man paused, and seemed to be weighing in his mind the argument of his subtle companion. It was evident from his countenance that the five hundred pounds was the difficulty which most oppressed him, if it can be supposed that the danger of possessing the proceeds of a burglary which was known throughout the country could have no influence on his judgment.

"I have not de monish," said be.

Job smiled.

"I will burn de cushed parshment."

"And by those means deprive Mr. Hindly of repaying you the sums you have already advanced on the estate to which those deeds refer. Think!"

"I tink I losh my monish," said he; "five hundred pound on deshe."

"They are the title deeds of Heathmoor, that is all," said Job, "stolen from the family mansion. Your possession of them may be innocent enough; but let me implore you to act consistently; burning them will do you no good, especially as you have no reason to do so on the score of danger."

" Danger ; why, share, you shaid it wash dan-
sherous to keep dem."

" That was only upon the supposition that you
couldn't account for the manner by which you
obtained them. Is the butterman a respectable
sort of person, or one not likely to come forward
to corroborate your statement? Suppose, now,
just for a moment, suppose that he got them
from the thief himself, is it likely that he will
voluntarily come forward in order to exonerate
you from the suspicion of having received stolen
property? Is it not more likely that he will run
away altogether as soon as the news reaches him
that they are discovered in your possession ?"

" But dey shall not be dishcovered—"

" No; but as an honest man you must give
them up; you dare not ruin the young man who
is justly entitled to them. Mr. Hindly is a friend
of mine, I have seen them, and I, for the sake of
my honour, could not permit him to suffer by
such foolery. I have acted as a friend between
you, and he is willing to deposit them with you

as security ; in plain terms, I must tell you, he knows you have them, but as he wants money he is more interested in winking at the matter than in prosecuting an enquiry as to the manner by which they have got into your hands. He is only too glad to hear they are safe."

" By de holy prophetsh," exclaimed Solomon.

" But this let me advise you," added Job, as he perceived that the moneymonger was ready to yield; "the matter must on no account be mentioned between you till the death of his father."

"Not mentioned!" said Solomon ; "not ashk for my monish?"

" No, not for your interest even. I will see to that."

Solomon looked aghast, and seemed incapable of comprehending the scheme of the ready-witted lawyer.

" He is supposed to know nothing of the matter, that these missing documents are the ones that were stolen. I will explain—with me, as his attorney, are deposited his deeds and documents; do you understand?"

" Yesh, yesh."

" I am commissioned to raise money on some of them, he doesn't know which, and doesn't care."

" But he knowsh I have deshe," said Solomon.

" Of course, but don't you see it would be like conniving at the robbery to acquiesce in—it would, in short, be making himself an accessory after the fact."

Solomon sighed a little, and once more turned to peruse the deed.

" It musht be ten per shent, not eight mind— not eight."

" It must be as I have put it," said Job ; " you must have what you can legally demand, five, which is there written."

" And you musht take two hundred for dish deed ?" said the Jew.

" I must take five hundred," answered Job, " as there written ; future advances may be conducted on more advantageous terms to yourself, as you please.   Your position will be better ; this, of course, Mr Hindly is aware of."

"Den you musht give me back fifty for luck," said the Jew.

"I must act according to my instructions," replied Job; and thus saying, looked at his watch, and requested a speedy settlement of the business, as a matter of graver importance demanded his presence elsewhere.

A few minutes only were necessary to produce and count the money, which Job carefully placed in his pocket-book, after which he left the money-lender in possession of the forged deed and the stolen parchments.

CHAPTER XII.

JOB ON MONEY AND MATRIMONY.

THE little affair recorded in the last chapter was one of the most inconsequential that Job had lately transacted ; but it suffices to show with what tact he was capable of turning every matter that presented itself before him to his advantage. "Small fish," said he, as he proceeded homewards, "are not to be despised." Moreover, his knowledge of the circumstance that the old man was in possession of stolen deeds, might be a powerful engine in his future dealings with the

money-lender. At present, however, he had other
matters in hand of a more important character.
As the reader will remember, he had devised a
scheme by which he could turn to ready money a
great deal of his father's landed property.   He
had already transferred much of it to himself by
means of forged deeds of gift from his father, and
a great deal had been disposed of under the supposed title which such deeds conferred.   Specu-
lators had purchased with an avidity characteristic
of the age of railway enterprise.   Buildings were
rising on the estates, and although the elder
Hawkins was shrewd for a man of his class, yet
he was easily deceived into the belief that all was
progressing in a manner perfectly consistent with
his interests.   A great deal of his property he
never saw ; he rather delighted to look upon the
ample returns which poured into his box through
the hands of his boy, and out of it again by the
same medium ; he was easily persuaded that,
where buildings rose upon his estate within the
scope of his limited observation, it was upon lands

comprised in such and such a building lease which he had granted. Thus he was kept in a constant state of satisfaction, as he saw before him the magnificent fortune which was rising under the auspices of his son.

Nor was Job by any means doubtful as to the result of the villainous deeds he was concocting. He had little doubt that he was the eldest son of him whom he had regarded with such filial veneration; and as his father had reposed in him such unbounded confidence, he had no reason to doubt that he would, at last, leave the good boy to take care of his mother and the younger scions of the family. A word about making his will had never been mentioned by either; and Job, with every regard for the law of primogeniture, was perfectly reconciled to the thought of being left fatherless whenever that event might happen. Mrs. Hawkins, it was true, in her frequent conferences with Job, had thrown out suggestions as to the propriety of a testament; but her dutiful son assured her it was not necessary—that there was no earthly reason why she should not have the sole use of the old man's property for her life, and afterwards, Job himself would take care that it was properly distributed. Had Job known that he was *nullius filius,* he might have taken a different view of the matter.

Mrs. Hawkins, however, with a mother's anxiety, prevailed upon her husband to perform the duty which devolved upon him, although the matter was kept a profound secret from the rest of the family. The lawyer who drew the will was a friend of Mrs. Hawkins, and had been summoned from Nottinghamshire, so that his knowledge of the property was by no means calculated to disturb the scheme which Job was pursuing of disposing of it before his father. Singularly enough, the estate, which was devised to "Job Hawkins, my natural son," the unnatural son had disposed of, the day before, at something like two-thirds of its real value. The portion of the eldest son, Richard, had already been carved out into plots, and was covered with villas. Some was in negotiation, and the rest only waited a purchaser.

The proceedings may appear strange to those acquainted with matters of business; but the reader must remember that Job was a lawyer versed in conveyancing; he had consequently every facility for the accomplishment of his purposes; he could get deeds engrossed, which, coming from the hands of any person not connected with the legal profession, would have excited suspicion and suggested enquiry. His father was almost bedridden, and left everything in the hands of his son. That son was a gentleman moving in the best society; a man of unblemished honour, of generous mind and liberal principles; a Member of Parliament, and notoriously the heir of one of the richest merchants in London. The deeds presented for the inspection of the purchaser's lawyers were *primâ facie* good, and gave no indication whatever of anything amiss. The only remarkable circumstance throughout the transactions, was, that not in one i nstance did it occur to any of the purchasers or their attorneys to visit the old man in order to ascertain whether the deeds of gift were genuine. But this would have been to throw a suspicion upon one who was above it. The conveyances were so well drawn, and the signature of the elder Hawkins so perfectly imitated, that no reasonable doubt could possibly suggest itself. The practice, it is true, was of so bold a character, that one can hardly imagine the equanimity with which the forger contemplated his actions. He had no doubt whatever of the result, and felt that if he sacrificed a large portion of the family estate, during the old man's life, he would have ample opportunity of making amends for it to the family after his decease, by the lustre which he would throw around the name, and the wealth which he himself would one day acquire. Ambition urged him forward, and whether it sent him to the precipice of ruin or the pinnacle of fame, all was to be encountered after he had taken his first step. So he proceeded.

It was a few nights after his last interview with

Solomon that Edgar presented himself at his house
in Mayfair, on his return from Heathmoor. Young
Hindly looked pale and careworn, and evidently
was suffering from that extreme agitation which
his peculiar circumstances would occasion. It was
a warm and hearty grasp of the hand that he received as Job welcomed him. Singularly enough,
Martha and Mary were there also, and with looks
beaming with kindness, expressed their gladness
at his return. They were visiting Job for the
purpose of obtaining from him a promise to put
down the slave-trade of the Southern States, with
a few other trifling matters, which they urged
upon the representative of their borough. Job
promised to do his best; he was hardly so sanguine
as his warm-hearted admirers, who were quite sure
his powerful eloquence (which, in the House, had
never gone beyond "hear, hear,") was destined
to achieve great things. Another matter which
they pressed upon their member with equal ardour,
was the bringing in a bill to abolish war. If he
could only get the duty off tea, too, it would be

such a nice thing. Martha also suggested that the soldiers, if they must be maintained at all, should be employed in the distribution of tracts. And Mary thought newspapers were a very bad thing, as tending to make people break the Sabbath, by reading them instead of their Bibles. All which matters, with sundry others, Job promised to attend to; and the damsels took their leave, gratified with the readiness with which he fell in with their views.

Edgar's congratulations were hearty, and were warmly reciprocated, after which the friends turned to the discussion of private matters. The adventures of Edgar to Heathmoor were narrated circumstantially and at length; after which Job rang the bell, and ordered Friday, who instantly made his appearance—for he was already listening at the key-bole—to bring cigars and wine, and two or three law-books, which he indicated by their bulk and position in the library.

"You see," said Job, "this is a case in which the law gives your father the property for his life;

at his death, no power on earth can prevent it from coming to you."

" Except," said Edgar, " that the newspapers say the title deeds, which I have reason to believe were in a certain cabinet, of which I have the key, were stolen in the late burglary. Of course you have heard of it !"

" Singular," said Job, puffing a long, thick cloud, and watching it as it dispersed itself over the ceiling.

" Yes, it's singular," replied Edgar, " that it should have taken place the very night after I left—nay, before I had fairly left the village."

" I don't know how the matter sits with you, Hindly," said Job, " but it strikes me very forcibly that the whole affair of the burglary is a mere pretence, and that the design was simply to obtain possession of the contents of that cabinet."

" In which case !" replied Edgar, " they need not have had recourse to the extreme measure of horsewhipping the inmates, Mr. Parchment in particular."

"I was not aware of that," replied Job; "nevertheless, that is scarcely an argument against the ruse to take the deeds."

"Moreover," added Edgar, "my father could have easily obtained them without any burglary at all; he had possession of the whole place."

"But not of the cabinet," interrupted Job; "that was a repository into which even he had no right to intrude; and since you have the key, depend upon it, the deeds are yet in the custody of your family.   Was there a marriage settlement?"

"Yes," answered Edgar, taking from his pocket a small packet of documents, which his mother had given him, and among which were the very articles of marriage from which the settlement should have been drawn.

"Ah!" exclaimed Job, "that's it—how—why —where did you get this?"

"It was lost," said Edgar, "and ever since my birth has been in my mother's possession till she gave it to me. I have reason to believe that my father will disinherit me; my mother felt that he would."

"But here," exclaimed Job, "is what will prevent even that. See, the estate of Raymonds is to be settled upon Amelia Morton and himself for life, and after their deaths to the first and other sons in tail male. Where are the trustees ?"

"The settlement never was made," said Edgar.

"The devil!" said Job; "that was foolery. We must fight this matter with the old man. Does he know of this document? Oh, you say he supposes it to have been lost, and upon that supposition intends to disinherit you. Whose signature is this?"

"Sir George Morton's."

"It's a curious signature," said Job, carefully

scrutinising it; "the devil could hardly imitate that if he wanted to. Are you sure?"

"Oh, yes; quite."

"Well, it's certainly the most curious writing I ever saw. Perhaps you will leave them with me, and I will peruse them at my leisure. Here's a letter I see from the old man to your mother respecting your marriage."

"Yes," replied Edgar, with a sigh; "I remember well the day that letter came. She had a hatred of that girl; but it's all over. I've stemmed the whole torrent of my father's wrath, and would defy the devil to make me have her now."

"Nay," said Job, "but it would be a jolly thing after all, to turn these fine sentiments into ready money, old fellow. Here is as good as a settlement. Old Walters will give you, of course, a sum proportioned to his daughter's ugliness, and there you are as square as a right angle. Why not marry her? Pay off your liabilities like a banker, and live like a prince. Two devilish pretty estates, plenty of money, and a wife that you need only have for company, holidays, and so forth. Marry, my boy, marry."

Edgar shook his head.

" Marry fire and water," said he.

" You think one will put the other out, eh ?"

" Had it not been for my father's foolery in trying to outshine the rest of his circle, there would never have been a thought of such a marriage ; but why should I pay his debts with my affections ?"

" Is Raymonds mortgaged ?" asked Job.

" To Sir Robert."

" And what of Heathmoor ?"

" I believe that, too, is encumbered ; at least, so I heard from Parchment."

" There's a devil of a difficulty in the whole matter," answered Job. " Of course your mother joined in the mortgage of Heathmoor ?"

" No doubt ; but how is the law upon that ?"

" Well, simply this, that you will be entitled
to have it redeemed out of your father's personalty, supposing the mortgage money was ap-
plied for his benefit; so that if he disinherits
you, there will still be a claim upon his assets."

" And with regard to Raymonds ?"

"That's rather a different matter, but I'm inclined to think that equity will compel him to
settle the estate according to the tenour of these
articles; if so, his personalty must again be had
recourse to to pay off the encumbrance."

" And if Sir Robert takes it into his head to
foreclose ?"

" Here's a kind of countervaling equity, at all
events," said Job, pointing to the articles; " but
as I said before, the matter is involved in difficulty, and if you could manage to make matters
comfortable without Chancery, it would be far
more profitable to all parties. Love is a very fine
thing, I admit; but, after all, it's the mere bloom
of matrimony, and the same sun that calls its
beauty into existence, withers it."

"I know nothing of that," said Edgar; "but if matrimony is worth a thought it's worth a heart. There are some—a great many, no doubt —who speculate in it as they would in anything else, and these persons, perhaps, act not very unwisely; they cannot be greatly the losers by their bargains, since they have no feelings that are capable of suffering, and no affections that are susceptible of injury. Marriage is their forlorn hope, a receipt in full for past profligacy, or, at least, a guarantee against the calls which would otherwise be made upon their energies;—'a covenant for quiet enjoyment,' in fact."

"Very good," said Job; "as you argue on my side, I must speak on yours, and certainly beauty, and love, and all that, are very nice and pleasant and enjoyable, and so are the Mayflowers, and winter sunshine, and butterflies' wings and the down of the peach; but—bah! there's nothing like the sterling gold, Hindly; it's the god of this world, say what you will, and he who lacks it, is but an ass for every fool to

ride and set his spurs in—why, a king without
money would be a beggar; and the more you
study life, the more plainly you will see that the
greater part of life's friendships are based on it,
respectability is covered with it, position depends
on it, and the world may as well be without the
sun as without money.   Why does the world pro-
fess to esteem me ?   Not because they have discovered in me anything intrinsically good, or
worthy of their admiration, but because my name
stands in its books with respectable sums at its
side.   It's the gift, not the giver, my friend, that
the world regards ; and the more you give, the
more they will respect.   Why, if Job Hawkins,
Esquire, M.P., stands upon the platform, the
audience is ready to shout ' hear, hear,' before I
speak ; but if Job Hawkins, without money or
position, were to stand before them, ten to one
but they would look upon him with contempt.
Gold !—money !—my friend, is all that the world
cares for; therefore, get money, though it's
sacked up in an ugly wife ; never mind, so long

as the sack's full—ha! ha! bravo, Job! was't always a good boy."

Edgar looked with something of surprise on his countenance as he listened to this wild burst of eloquence. There was certainly a marked difference between Mr. Hawkins on the platform and Mr. Hawkins in his private character.

" You seem surprised," he continued; " but mix with the world, my dear fellow, and the world will soon convince you that its practical philosophy, and its theoretical philosophy, are two vastly different matters. Life's dreamy poetry is one thing, and its stiff prose another. You men of poetical temperament, see fantastic visions that will never be realised; the world itself is a reality —you make it a dream. Love and beauty are all very well to write about, but they are as unsatis-fying as the dreams of a hungry man who fancies himself at a feast."

"I don't agree with you," said Edgar; " to me it matters little what god is the object of the world's idolatry. If I do not bow down to it it is no divinity of mine; it is true, my experience has been chiefly confined to the profligacy of life, which has been fed by the hand of craving money-mongers. I have sold my birth-right for a mess of pottage, and must content myself with my bargain, but abandon *all* to the world I will not. There is something in life worth hoping for, beyond the mere gratification of an hour, and I feel that there are affections to be cherished, hopes to be fostered—ah! smile if you like—and virtue to be cultured. Life is neither money nor pleasure; it consists in a realisation of its solemn duties, and their punctual performance; in the pursuit of truth and the fulfilment of obligations which we owe to a greater god than gold.

" And your pursuit of truth, and fulfilment of these divine obligations," answered Job, " are to be summed up in the delicious craving which you have for the beauty of a poor homeless girl, who has nothing in the world to recommend her to your notice and affection, but her face."

" There you err, and wrong the girl too," said Edgar.

" How ?"

" Her beauty is the least of her attractions," answered Edgar.

" If it's less than her fortune," replied Job, " it's a worse set off-than I expected."

" She has mind," said Edgar.

" I never thought you'd be fool enough to fall in love with a lunatic, Hindly. Of course she has mind, so has Lucy."

" And a soul," said Edgar.

" Or she couldn't be immortal; her pretty person, however, will soon fade, wear out as you look at it—presto—quick—begone—says the great juggler Time. And where is it? it may be in Heaven for ought you know, but that's no satisfaction. Bah! Hindly, marry Lucy, and you shall have that which will make the world worship you. However, if you're bent on ruin, I cannot help it. Why the devil can't you marry Lucy, and—retain—ah—well—no matter."

" Say on," said Edgar.

" It was a momentary thought," answered Job ;

"what I mean is, if you don't like Lucy you might leave her."

"True," said Edgar; "marry her, in short, simply to plunder her."

"Heaven forbid, my dear fellow; you have a monarch for your example. You are in debt and difficulties; you want money, and have nothing to retrieve your position but these papers and a reversionary interest in one estate, which is already swallowed up by mortgage debts, and those debts owing to the man who will give you the whole sum, and throw his daughter into the bargain."

"I don't care," said Edgar; "I mean to marry Lizzy, though Misfortune herself is the bridesmaid."

"And the devil is the parson," said Job. "Well, well, old boy, I wish you success, and will drink to it with a full tumbler. As for these deeds, if you will leave them in my hands I will go through them carefully, and if anything can be done in the matter I will do it for you, old fellow. Come, you don't drink; this rusticating has made a boy of you; but I suppose you want, or will want, some of the old stuff?"

" I shall want but very little," said Edgar, " for I'm going into a merchant's office."

" The devil's office," said Hawkins. " What do you want in a merchant's office?"

" I mean it," answered Edgar.

" You can get money on these," said Job, " if you wish it."

" I am sick of mortgages, and bills, and bonds," replied Edgar.

" Why so am I," replied Job; " but you know the old saying ' needs must,' &c. My governor's laid up in lavender, and until he dies I have nothing; consequently I am obliged to follow the old practice: it would scarcely do for me to wait till so uncertain an event before I set sail on the ' tide of my affairs.' I took it at the flood, and here I am, you see, making way like a seventy-four in a stiff breeze. Get into Parliament, old boy—

liberalism, that's the dodge now-a-days. Here's old Macbeth, as we call him in the House, just about to accept the Chiltern Hundreds. What say you to going in for the seat? You're a county fellow, you know—old family."

"No," said Edgar; " that might have been my ambition at one time, but the tide that you caught at the full, is dead against me. If I can just moor alongside some good old pier—"

"You mean p e e r," said Job; " that 'll do— and that you will do if you only take my advice."

"If I can just keep myself from going down, that is all I wish at present," said Edgar, " matters may turn."

"And if I can only keep myself going up," " that's all I want. Now, you know it's a faint heart that can't get over an obstacle or two; there's no credit in swimming *with* the tide, the difficulty is in pushing ahead against it: I wouldn't give a straw for the fame that's won without an effort. It's my glory to think that I have planted my ladder upon my own foundation, instead of my father's; if I had waited till the money tumbled in, it would have been easy enough—there would have been success to start with. But I'm a sort of bold adventurer, Hindly; like Columbus, who only guessed there was another world, and set sail to find it."

"But it strikes me, Hawkins," said Edgar, "that you scarcely know to what extent you are involved—these undertakings, splendid as they all are, have not been done without an extravagant outlay."

"That's true, Hindly; but I don' care a straw —when the bark's near making shipwreck, as mine has been so often, the captain has little scruple about throwing overboard the cargo. My man Friday knows as much about my real position as I do myself. It may seem extraordinary that I should not have imitated the wise king before he made war, but I didn't; young and ambitious, I disregarded the means for the sake of

the end—but this I know, that by and bye I shall
be all right."

" If your debt don't exceed your fortune."

" That can hardly be.   Come, Hindly, another
glass."

" No more," said Edgar.   " I must wish you
good-night ; when shall I see you ?"

" Any day, old fellow—call every day—if I am
not here—by the bye, will you come down to ' the
house' to-morrow evening ; there's rather an interesting matter coming on."

Edgar assented, and, warmly returning the
hearty grasp of the hand which Job gave him,
took his leave.

It is hardly possible to conceive the extreme
buoyancy of spirit which, even when alone, Job
manifested—and yet there were occasions, when a
tinge of anxiety was apparent on his handsome
countenance.   He was hardly ever depressed, for
his very determination and recklessness saved
him from that ; indeed, had he allowed melancholy to master him, his position would have been

fearful in the extreme. Job possessed the phy-
sical qualities of a thorough rogue, heartless in
his purposes, and regardless as to who might be
the victims of his unbridled extravagance. His
pace was dreadful, by far too rapid for him either
to note the landmarks of his journey as the
world swept along beneath him, or to contemplate the goal. Up to a recent period in his
career, he had consoled himself with the thought
that he had risked no one's property but his own,
but as estate after estate disappeared from his
father's property, he must have been less shrewd
than people believed, if he did not perceive that
he had disposed of a greater portion of the estates
than would fall to his share should his father not
die intestate. But it was various other little in-
vestments which Job merely appropriated for the
time being, and which he at first hoped to be able
to restore, that turned the balance of his moral
reasoning, and overthrew his conscientious scru-
ples. It was true, the interest of Martha's and
Mary's stock was as regularly paid, as though it

had remained in the original " three per cents. ;" but all concern about the right or the wrong of his substituting shares in a company, as a security for the money, which he had first invested and then drawn out in his own name, was gone. It was beyond dispute, that the elderly damsels received more money per quarter than they had been accustomed to, but it was equally true that the principal was gone. For the present we leave Martha and Mary in blissful ignorance of their true estate, and return to the contemplation of the more lively character who stood so high in their estimation.

When Edgar had left his friend, Job flung himself into his chair, and, placing one foot on the hob and the other on the mantel-piece, gave way to his reflections, which, crowding upon him as they did, allowed little opportunity to examine any particular circumstance which occasioned them : it was rather the general effect of his circumstances that Job contemplated than any single matter. They might be likened to the

spokes of a wheel, which, revolving with extreme
rapidity, left no time, or afforded no opportunity,
for examining any spoke in particular; the
" whole thing," as Job would say, seemed pretty
correct, and he had little doubt would be all right
by and bye. The honble. member was seldom in
the habit of expressing himself aloud when alone ;
but on this occasion he broke through his usual
rule, and from his disconnected exclamations the
following monologue may be gathered :—" Well,
friend Hindly, if *you* won't mortgage *I* will. Now,
here are the signatures of the old squire and the
worthy baronet, but it's a devilish curious piece of
penmanship, this ' Robert Walters ;' why a hen
would scratch as good a signature as that. Let
me see—let me see, Job, a piece of thin paper
will do that little trick, so that old Walters would
be afraid of committing perjury, if he should deny
the handwriting—cunning old dog! Now, Sir
Robert, I shall take the liberty of mortgaging
your estate for you—there have been such things
done without the title deed: I can account for

them to old Gregory, and Gregory can account
for them to his client. As for these articles of
marriage, why it's likely enough that I can draw
the settlement; and then, with Hindly's signature, raise enough wind to fill a sail, should I
happen to be becalmed before the governor has his
next apopletic. Ha! ha! ha! ha—capital fellow; wast always a good boy Job. I can square
at last—redeem the mortgages, replace Martha
and Mary's stock, and, perhaps, make their will.
Ha! ha! O dear, dear—what a lark!"

Thus saying, Job retired to his bedroom.

CHAPTER XIII.

MRS. ELDERLY'S ACCOUNT OF THE BURGLARY.

EDGAR's position was one of extreme difficulty. Clouds gathered on every side, and evil seemed to threaten him from every quarter. Nor were his anxieties confined to his own circumstances; there was one who was suffering on his account, and of whom he could get no tidings. It was impossible to settle his mind to any course, whatever plans he projected, until he should discover her for whom he had sacrificed so much. To abandon Lizzy after all he had endured for her sake, and after all she must have suffered for his, would be to cast away the prize for which he had struggled so severely. Once more, therefore, he determined upon returning to Heathmoor. His implicit confidence in Job, led him to believe that he would exert himself to the utmost on his account; and if there was a possibility of success, he felt certain that no energies would be spared on the part of his friend to achieve it. That his father had acted the part of a tyrant—nay, that he had defrauded him of his rights, he felt convinced. The marriage articles had luckily been preserved, and upon them rested his last hope of regaining the position he had abandoned.

A compromise might be effected; and, with this view, he instructed Job to write to his father, setting forth the circumstances, and demanding a fulfilment of the anti-nuptial arrangement. By this line of policy, Job was saved from at least one of the dangerous measures which he contemplated; and, after remonstrating with Edgar upon the subject, wrote the letter and despatched it to Raymonds.

The surprise and mortification of Hindly may be imagined; his own cupidity was disclosed, and in the madness of his fury, he accused his deceased wife of the most shameless treachery, and his son of the burglary. Rumours had already reached his ears that Edgar was suspected, that his presence at Heathmoor on the night of the robbery had been sworn to, that he had been seen in company with the gipsies the evening before; now came the corroborative circumstance that he was in possession of papers that could have come from no other place than the cabinet at Heathmoor.

But the pride of Hindly overcame his feelings of revenge. Although he felt assured of his son's participation in the crime, the charge must be refuted rather than confirmed. His rage was beyond bounds; he threw the letter into the fire and snatched it back. He knew that an explanation was necessary to screen him from the

censure of those who would but too readily put
the worst construction upon the circumstance.
But he felt also that his son was a villain, and
the more he contemplated his supposed triumph,
the less he felt inclined to do him justice. Parchment was yet at Heathmoor, and, without delay,
he resolved on a journey to the Abbey.

As he rode into the wilderness which surrounded that once splendid estate, a strange and
overpowering sensation came over him; he felt
as he alone can feel to whom the world presents
no living object of regard, to whose memory
beings, once loved, recur with hatred instead of
affection, and to whom even the solace of sympathy is denied.

There was little ceremony in the manner of his
introduction to Mr. Parchment, who was in his
chamber, and scarcely able to rise from the
effects of the late maltreatment.   A glance was
sufficient to reveal to the representative of the
law, that Mr. Hindly's feelings were far from
composed.

"Have you found the rascals?" he demanded. Parchment raised his hands.

"Have you found them?" repeated Hindly.

"They have found the cabinet," said Parchment.

"Where?—it may afford a clue."

"It was on the common, and strange to say, Mr. Hindly, unbroken—unbroken, sir."

"Unbroken!" exclaimed Hindly; "then it cannot be—my son has had no share in this matter. Thank Heaven, I am spared this last sorrow that can befall a father's heart. I thought that one who bore the name of Hindly, would never disgrace it thus; now I can forgive him all the rest. Are you sure—sure, Parchment?"

And the father's eyes filled with tears as he awaited the lawyer's reply. Till that moment he did not know that he had the least affection left. But what can banish a parent's love? or what obliterate the tender memories that bring back the hours of prattling childhood? A thousand years might roll away, and a thousand oceans separate parent and child, but the memory of happy days would float like music over the wilds of time, and survive the tumult of the loudest storms.

"I hope he's not guilty," said Parchment.

"Hope!" exclaimed Hindly; "then you fear he is?"

"Nay," replied the lawyer, "but circumstances—"

"Speak! what circumstances do you mean? None, surely, that can connect him with guilt like this?"

"He told me he would have the cabinet," said Parchment.

"It is nothing."

"And the key!—the key!"

"What of the key, Parchment? Speak! tell me—is he apprehended? My God! why don't you tell me?"

"The key was in the cabinet," said Parchment; "Thornbury saw him with the gipsies the night before, and Thornbury swears to him as being in the house at the time."

The old man trembled; a sickening sensation

overpowered him, and he leaned for support on the massive oaken chair near which he stood, and his heart seemed ready to burst from his bosom. He staggered round the chair, and as he fell back into it, a cold perspiration came over him; he threw his hands upon his face and sobbed. How changed from what he was when he left Raymonds. Who was to be forgiven now—himself or his son?

" Where is this Thornbury?" he asked, after a long and painful pause.

" He is hereabouts," replied Parchment; " but let me assure you, Mr. Hindly, that, strong as this circumstantial evidence is to warrant suspicion, sir, I have little idea that your son can be a participator in such a crime, sir. Thornbury, however, has deposed to the facts, and the matter rests chiefly upon his evidence, together with—with the circumstance of the key. Who could have had the key of the cabinet, sir, but— but your son?"

" God forgive me!" said Hindly.

" Forgive *you*, my dear sir," said Parchment ; "you have nothing to reproach yourself with, come what may of the affair. Bad company, sir, bad connections, always lead to mischief."

" Is Thornbury here ?" asked Hindly, with a one of anger that at once ended the moralising strain into which Parchment was drifting. "Where is the housekeeper? Is there no one here, in Heaven's name, but you, Parchment ?"

He rose suddenly, and pulled the bell with such violence, that it resounded through the house.

Mrs. Elderly entered, dressed in her best gown, which hung straight down her person, while over her bosom met the edges of two large flaps like those of an ancient tippet. A cap, with an immense border, encircling her whole face, was carefully adjusted and tied with blue ribbons under her chin. She curtseyed low as she entered, and again as she advanced towards the Squire, then stood to receive his orders.

" Is Thornbury here ?" asked Hindly.

"Yes, sir, if you please," said Elderly, as she gave another bob.

"Send him to me," said Hindly; "but stay—were you here on the night of the robbery?"

"O, yes, I were, indeed, sir, if you please; and—and—I have never been myself since."

"Never been what?" demanded Hindly, fiercely.

"Never been the thing since."

"What do you mean by never been the thing; do you know who did it?"

"No, sir," said Elderly.

"Did you see the burglars?"

"Oh, yes, sir; they looked right into our bed, they did, and I were in that fright—"

"Looked into your bed?"

"Yes, sir; I mean—that is, I should ha' said they looked through the curtings at us; but fust of all, sir, I hears a noise, and I says, says I to Didcot, that's the housemaid, sir, I says, says I, 'lor, Didcot,' I says, 'whatever's that?' and then we listened and both eeard, and Didcot jumps up and she says, says she, 'whatever *can* it be?' she says."

"Now, Mrs. Elderly," interposed Parchment, "Mr. Hindly is not asking what you said."

"Do you know who the men were?" asked Hindly.

"Lor, sir, they had crape on their faces, and sich orrid looks as I never *can* forget."

"Did they speak?"

"They said, sir—I mean one on 'em says, sir, says he 'lay still, you old b——,' says he, but I don't like to say, sir, what they said; it was a awful word."

"They told you to lie still."

"And Didcot hollered, and then one on 'em clapped a plaster on her mouth."

"And what then? did they ask you for any keys?"

"Lor, no, sir."

"Nor yet where anything was kept?"

" No, sir; but they said how if we moved a limb they'd cut us in half. Oh, sir, it wur a awful night, that wur."

" Where was Thornbury ?"

" He wur asleeping in the next room ; and to ear his cries, sir ! Oh, dear, they seemed to go through me; and Didcot says, says she ' they're a murderin' of Thornbury, and he's drunk.' "

" Drunk !" said Hindly ; " was he drunk ?"

" No, sir; he worn't to say drunk, though he had had a drop to drink."

" Go on; what became of them after this ?"

" We eeard 'em a ransackin' the place, and after a bit they goes away ; and then we ears Thornbury a groanin' in one room, and this ere gentleman in another. So we goes, and there they was tied up to the bedposts like as if they was crucified."

At this moment Thornbury entered. There was a look of villany on his coarse, unshaven face, which was almost fiendish; his eyes peered beneath his low forehead, and glanced at Hindly as though they would reach his innermost thought; but the look that was returned sufficiently indicated the feeling of the indignant squire, and was at once a caution and a reproof.

"Thornbury!" said Hindly, "you charge my son with being a participator in this robbery."

"I ain't, sir," replied Thornbury.

Hindly looked at Parchment.

"I telled the magistrate what I see," continued Thornbury, "and what I can swear to; he wor wi' the gipsies the night afore the robbery, on the common, and he told this 'ere gentleman and me that he would have them papers. This 'ere gentleman 'eerd him as well as me; he told us as how he'd got the key, and the box wor found unlocked, with the key in it; and it's my bleef he wor one as wor in the house at the time."

"Why is it your belief? You were drunk on that night?"

"I worn't, sir."

" Mrs. Elderly ?" said Hindly.

" No, sir ; I didn't say as how he wor drunk ; it wur Didcot, sir."

" Didcot's a liar," said Thornbury. " Didcot wur drunk, and you too."

" There !" exclaimed Elderly, " only think o' that ! Why there's a good-for-nothin' willin ! Why, sir, he were that tipsy he couldn't stand."

" You may go," said Hindly ; " and as for you, Thornbury, you can leave here immediately. Your charge is false."

" We shall see," replied the keeper, " may be I shall be one too many for un yet. I means to say, sir, as how I can swear to 'em all ; for it ain't the fust time I 'ave seen these here gipsies he wor with."

Thus saying, Thornbury left the room.

" I am afraid, sir," said Parchment, " there's too much reason to apprehend that your son was implicated. I don't mean to say a participator in the business. Accessory, sir, before the fact ;

but we must rebut the evidence; you see, sir, the principal witness was drunk; but then, again, the circumstances, as I said before, are so very strong. Here is the key—the key, sir, which is a very important link in the chain. A particular key, you see, sir, with certain initials on it."

" Great Heaven !" exclaimed Hindly, " l remember the key. Why did you not give up the papers ?"

And as Hindly spoke he wrung his hands in the agony of despair. A feeling of inexpressible horror overwhelmed him, and a dizzy sensation seemed to consume his brain.

" He had better have married the veriest scullion," he continued ; " anything would have been better than this. My God ! that I should have lived to this hour ! Parchment, take charge of my affairs ; everything shall be sold, and I will leave this place."

Even Parchment, whose heart was as free from the finer feeling of humanity as a heart could well be, could not behold the agony of the father without emotion.   Such anguish, such unutterable despair he had never seen before.

"My dear, sir," said he, "let us wait the sequel. We don't know yet how things may turn out. Edgar may have left the country ; if so, the disgrace you contemplate is spared ; and even if he remain, and should be apprehended upon the warrant, there may, after all, be a lack of evidence."

"Evidence!" exclaimed Hindley. "You yourself are a witness against him, sir."

"Heaven forbid," replied Parchment. "Leave the case in my hands, sir. Neither skill nor pains shall be wanting."

"You say he told you he would have the papers, which you refused to give up."

"Ay, sir ; but that does not amount to an absolute threat of committing a burglary. He did say so ; but that circumstance may be turned in his favour, sir ; he said it in a passion, sir—idle words, perhaps."

"It's no use, Parchment. Heaven forgive me ! I have wronged the boy, and driven him to ruin ;

he was a noble hearted youth, and I was proud to call him my son. My cursed fortune caused me to plan a marriage for him that he rejected. It has returned upon me, Parchment, and I reap the harvest I have sown. Poor Edgar ?"

And as the old man spoke he covered his face with his hands, and the tears streamed from his cheeks, while the sobs seemed almost to choke him. His thoughts were like the visions of some unhappy dream, indistinct and horrible. In those few moments were focussed the events of a life. The image of his wife stood before him as his accuser. She who had been so fond and so proud of her child seemed to return from her solemn sleep, as though the disgrace and ruin of her boy had disturbed her in the tomb.

There is no censure more painful than that which conscience inflicts. Enemies may calumniate, and friends reprove, but of all reproaches our own are the worst to endure. They fall like the lash of justice, untempered with mercy. Rack the brain for an excuse, but invention fails; and even the punishment itself neither atones for the guilt nor passes it away. At such times friends, even enemies, are more merciful than our own hearts. Nothing can palliate the wrong, and nothing alleviate the pang. Conscience, unendurable conscience, wraps us in flames of fire such as our tears cannot quench.

So felt Hindly; his conscience seeming to throb as it accused him of his son's ruin. There was nothing that could solace, no one who could persuade him he was guiltless. The incrustation of pride was broken through by the bolt of conscience, and the devils of his own heart arose, horrifying him with their hideous forms, and tormenting him with the evils of a mis-spent life.

CHAPTER XIV.

ENCOMPASSED WITH DANGERS.

LIZZY's gentle nature and amiable disposition prevented her from taking those measures for her safety, against Thornbury, which prudence might have suggested.

Her situation was dangerous in the extreme. She had been in daily apprehension of encountering the malignant enemy who was evidently bent upon her destruction. The more she reflected upon the circumstances of that awful night, when she was so providentially rescued by the gipsy, the more she dreaded a recurrence of the scene.

But when she quitted Heathmoor with her mother,
they directed their steps towards a distant village on the sea shore, where, many years ago,
Mrs. Wilmington had stayed, having taken up
her abode at the cottage of a fisherman, whose
wife she had known in better days.

The old lady and her husband were still alive,
and gladly welcomed their friend and her daughter. Not long after their arrival a letter, apparently in Edgar's handwriting, was left at the
cottage by a stranger.

The contents were brief, as though hurriedly
written, and appointed a time and place of meeting on the sea beach. The handwriting was so
like Edgar's, and the language so endearing, that
Lizzy's excessive joy left no room for doubt; and
as the meeting was arranged for an hour before
night fall, the too credulous girl set out on her
journey of expected happiness.

The moon shone resplendently on the waters of
the beautiful bay of ——, the light, fleecy clouds
floated with a motion scarcely perceptible, and

the tide, as it rolled its curling waves upon the beech, seemed conscious of the glorious scene; one might almost have imagined that it poured itself upon the shore as gently as possible, lest it should disturb the sweet serenity of that gorgeous evening. Lizzy was the only living being visible, as the silvery twilight heightened the effect of the picture. Hopefully she wandered along the beach, watching now the curling crests of the ever restless surges, now looking eagerly in the direction of the projecting cliff in the distance. But as the twilight deepened, her thoughts seemed to receive the shadow of its darker hue; and feelings, almost melancholy, made her bosom throb more quickly as she wandered on.

"He loves me," she thought, "and yet it is a love which cannot be acknowledged. The world must know nothing of it, and I am to be his wife, but no one is to know it but ourselves. Well, it doesn't matter about the world knowing it, the world couldn't add anything to our joy, and fine people would only look down upon me, even as Edgar's wife. I would rather not go among fine people. I shall be as happy as one can be in this world."

In spite of Lizzy's reasoning, there was a tinge of unhappy foreboding in her thoughts. Why, she knew not, but the very arguments she used, whenever she thought of the marriage, were proofs of an apprehension which she could neither understand nor believe. By this time she had reached the place mentioned in the letter. Edgar was not there. It was the first time she had known him fail to keep his word, and a slight misgiving momentarily disturbed her. She did not doubt his love, and instantly an apology for his absence suggested itself.

She seated herself upon a projecting crag, and gave herself up to the thousand reflections that crowded her brain. Sometimes she thought it was foolish to have loved him; then she remembered how he had often said that love made all equal; how he had pledged his very soul, and called Heaven to witness, that his heart was sincere. She could not now, she never had doubted him.

An hour had passed, and Lizzy was about to return, when a footstep caused her to pause; from what direction the sound came it was impossible to say, but a footstep it undoubtedly was. She listened, and a slight fear for a moment unnerved her—she was far from the cottage, and entirely defenceless; the loneliness of her position reproached her with the impropriety of venturing so far at such a time, and for the first time in her life, she accused Edgar of unkindness. There was another step, and it seemed as if someone were descending the cliff above her head, although no one was visible; her heart shuddered, her blood seemed to stagnate, and a cold shiver ran through her veins; she looked wildly around, but still there was not a living object to be seen. Suddenly the moon threw its radiance upon the cliffs above her, and a shadow was then visible, the shadow of a man it appeared, but where the person himself was, she could not perceive; she felt a choking sensation of fear; and even in the dreadful excitement of that moment, forgot to use the only means of safety which were available; her eyes were fixed upon the shadow, which distinctly portrayed the figure of a man in a bending or crouching attitude; it was motionless, and the dreadful thought suggested itself that the man was watching her from behind some projecting crag. The thought was more appalling, as the distinctness of the shadow indicated that the figure was but a short distance off. She was about to turn and run, but almost as soon as she had withdrawn her eyes from the spot, they fixed themselves on it again; her brain became dizzy, and excessive fright seemed at last to destroy even the power of thought; she stood like one half awake, half asleep, gazing upon some horrid vision which had disturbed the slumber.

A cloud had passed over the moon, and the shadow was no longer visible; the half bewildered girl turned from the cliff, and with a speed which only the apprehension of impending danger could impart, she rushed along the beach in the direction of the cottage; but it was a long, long way off, and, as the poor girl, half distracted, arrived at a spot where the steep cliff jutted out upon the beach, a sudden shriek burst from her lips, a wild cry of despair, for the waters were already dashing with loud fury upon the chalky wall (a sudden wind having sprung up), and Lizzy saw that her hope of escape by the route she had taken, was cut off. The waves, as if triumphing in her helpless flight, dashed nearer and nearer to her at every swell, rolling and foaming with increasing fury, till it seemed as if the flood were only advancing for the purpose of her destruction. She clasped her hands as she looked upon the waves that lashed the projecting cliff, and cried to Heaven for mercy. She crept close to the rock, and endeavoured to wade through the waters with the hope of reaching the other side before the tide was at its full, for the thought had already crossed her mind that her last hope must be to climb the cliff, upon which she had seen the shadow. At that point alone, along the whole beach, was there the possibility of escaping.

The tide was still rising, and every wave as it swelled and burst, seemed to threaten her with destruction. Lizzy had a brave heart, but she

had also the weakness of her sex, and it was
not for her delicately formed limbs to stem the
flood that dashed against her with redoubled
fury every moment; it was a struggle for
life even where she was; a single step might
be destruction; her only course was to return,
but even that was difficult. However, by dint of
extraordinary exertion, she once more reached the
yet remaining portion of the beach which the
waves had not invaded; but her terrors were not
over, the shadow on the cliff was an omen which
filled her with despair; the very absence of Edgar
was portentous. The letter came to her mind, it
might not be *his*,—it might, nay it must be a plot
to inveigle her into some unhappy dilemma.
Heaven! what a feeling of alarm choked her
bosom! Each moment the waves drove her nearer
and nearer to the dreaded spot, and the apprehensions of a thousand evils threw their gloom upon
her mind. Whoever the being might be that
lurked upon the cliff, he must have known that
escape by the path she had taken was impossible;

if he designed ill, he was exulting in the prospect
of its accomplishment. Her heart sank—alone,
defenceless, without the possibility of escape, and
surrounded by danger.

There was a little inlet in the cliff, midway
between the jutting point from which she had
retreated, and the spot which she dreaded to
approach; towards this cavern, for so it might be
termed, she hastened, for there was just the
probability that the tide did not rise very high
within it, and if it were possible to await till the
flood receded, although immersed waist high, it
would be better than venturing upon the horrible
danger which seemed to threaten her. But the
heavens were blackening with clouds, and the
moon was lower; the cave would be dark; at all
events, scarcely light enough to enable her to
discover the height to which the flood usually
rose. She proceeded towards it, cautiously and
timidly, her very footsteps appeared to her like
those of a pursuer, and every crash of the angry
ocean sounded like the voice of doom. Suddenly she stopped. Whether it was imagination

or whether a dreadful reality appeared before her she could not tell. A faint shriek passed her lips, and she sank upon the shore : some minutes the poor girl remained in her fixed and motionless position, and it was not till the waves had washed over her that she awoke to a state of consciousness. She then saw the face of a man suddenly protruded from behind the projecting side of the cavern and as quickly withdrawn ; she looked for a moment in the direction of the distant point where she had hoped to meet Edgar, but nothing was visible save the long curving line of foam that surged upon the beach.

The head once more protruded from the cave ; Lizzy shrieked, and her shriek was answered with a shout of laughter, as the tall figure of a man emerged from the cavern. His garments were disposed loosely about his person, as though for the purpose of concealing rather than clothing it. One hand was enfolded in the cloak that hung about his shoulders, while the other seemed to gather the folds of its skirt more closely about him; a slouched hat was drawn far over his forehead, and almost concealed the eyes which gleamed below its brim.

" What do you want ?" shrieked Lizzy.

The man seemed for a moment to consider what reply he should return—his formidable appearance, if not his manner, was enough to strike terror into a bolder heart than that of a woman; but this evidently did not enter his mind, even if his intentions were honest.

" Do you want to be *drownded?*" he asked, " don't yer see that the tide's coming in and there's no gittin' away except by the cliff there, which is a good mile to the westard, and I ain't sure as even there you ain't cut off; you'd better come into this ere cave, for a storm is lowering, and if yer goes to do the foreland yer'll be lost."

" I will try," said Lizzy, " I can run, and it is not so far—besides, Mr. Hindly is to meet me here."

Lizzy spoke, but her forebodings can hardly be imagined from her words; it was a forced courage which she assumed. A sudden presence of mind prompted her to speak of Edgar's coming to meet her, but it served no purpose with the man before whom she stood.

" Mr. Hindly ! " said he. " You're fool enough then to bleeve in genlemen like him ; do yer think such fine birds goes out on such nights as these ?"

" He will be *here* presently," said Lizzy.

" But I tell yer the tide's up, my putty bird, and no one can't get round the foreland now. See, you are knee deep, aready !" And as he spoke he put forth his hand to take Lizzy's, as if to lead her further from the advancing waves ; she drew back, and at the same moment a heavy wave meeting her, dashed her headlong upon the beach. All hope now forsook her ; she was at the mercy of the man who stood over her, and that his purposes were villainous, every word and every look gave her cause to apprehend. She felt his arm round her, and the contact seemed to impart courage and strength ; instantly she grappled, slender as she was, with the big, broad shouldered ruffian who enclasped her.

" Leave me ! leave me !" she exclaimed.

" Coward! leave me, I say—if you seek my death, save yourself the guilt of murder, and let the waves—"

" No! no!" interrupted the man ; " but you shall go with me to this 'ere cave, and there we can stay till the ebb, and then you can go."

" No!" shrieked Lizzy, " I will not ! I will not!"

" I don't mean no harm, gal!"

" Then let me go !" shrieked Lizzy.

" You shall go my way fust," said the ruffian, attempting to drag her to the cave; " it's my way fust, and your own arter, my sweet bird."

There was a fearful struggle—Lizzy seemed suddenly endowed with tremendous strength—for some time she even forced her antagonist further from the cliff; and although the waves were surrounding them, the determined girl withstood his endeavours to drag her to the cave.

Suddenly he paused, and holding her firmly by the arms, said—

" I don't mean yer no 'arm ; why don't yer come with me ?   I want to speak to yer about Edgar."

" Heaven have mercy on me !" cried the exhausted girl; and, as she spoke, fell back into the surge, dragging the ruffian with her—for the position was by no means easy to stand in, even without the difficulty of supporting another. The waves seemed to come faster and higher than ever, and now, with the tenacity of a drowning person, the unhappy girl clung to her enemy; below the surface of the waves the struggle was renewed. Lizzy's hands clenched firmly the clothes of the fiend who was upon her, and every moment increased the danger of both; but the wretch, rendered desperate, made a violent effort to escape. As he did so, the body of his victim rose to an almost perpendicular position; her arms were straight and stiff, as if with the rigidity of death, and in horror he looked at her pale face and glaring eyes; her fingers still held his garment, and all his efforts to unclench them seemed vain. Terror, at last, seized the cowardly brute; he shuddered; his blood ran cold, and his only desire now was to hasten his escape from the scene. "Alone with the dead!" was a thought past endurance, and the dead glaring at him with ghastly eyes in the dim moonlight, clinging to him with the tenacity of a vice.

At length he disengaged that portion of the vestment to which she clung. The next difficulty was to escape—for the tide was nearly at its full, and the ordinary means were cut off. To climb the cliff, under other circumstances, would have appeared madness; but the bewilderment under which the wretched man laboured was little short of insanity; and anything—everything, indeed, must be attempted rather than remain in a position so awful and so dangerous. Should he wait till the tide should have receded, he would probably be detected. Throwing away, therefore, the remaining portion of the cloak, he commenced the perilous attempt to climb the cliff, which, to the height of a hundred and fifty feet, rose almost perpendicularly. A few yards, however, from the fatal spot, there was a part of the chalky steep known to the neighbourhood as the "Devil's Pathway," and to which tradition had ascribed the singular quality of ensuring from all future danger and difficulty, whoever should succeed in gaining the summit by that perilous path. There was a legend also of a young fisherman, who once ascended it, to the effect that some years afterwards, throwing himself from its summit, in a fit of desponding love, he was transformed into a seagull in his descent. Whether this was in verification of the traditionary superstition, I know not; but the legend, and the wonderful quality ascribed to the " Devil's Pathway," gained great credence in the neighbouring village.

The ruffian had no sooner disengaged himself from his burden, than a feeling of compassion— or perhaps remorse—came over him—even reason seemed to exercise a sway more powerful than she in general does under similar circumstances. He looked a moment upon the pale, calm features of the girl, and a sob burst from his lips. There she lay, quiet enough now—she, who had struggled so desperately a short time ago for her honour ; there was no resistance now; do what you will with her helpless body; you can scoop out a grave for her in yonder cave, and as the flood washes over her, no one will know that she lies there. You can fling her farther out into the deep, to be drawn down with the tide or washed away. But, no; there is something akin to compassion even in that wicked heart, as he looks for a moment into those mysterious eyes—eyes that once kindled with all the beautiful emotions of woman, now awful in their solemnity; of the same soft blue as heretofore, but reflecting intolerable wrath.

"Nay!" exclaimed the miserable wretch, "I didn't mean yer no harm, poor gal. I didn't come to kill yer."

He stooped to take hold of her, in order to carry her to the cave, that the sea might not break over her; but a sudden horror returned upon him as he touched her—a shock, more powerful than electricity, unnerved him; and, staring for a moment wildly at the girl, he fled to the spot where he felt that his only hope of safety was. Alas! for hope that is the offspring of despair!

CHAPTER XV.

NOT LOST.

LIZZY was not dead ; but the excitement, and the
extraordinary efforts she had made, had exhausted
her.   Her spirit was unsubdued, but her delicate
system could endure no longer—she had swooned ;
and, indeed, to all appearance, life had departed.
After the man had left her, she lay for some time
prostrate and motionless ; the waves came nearer
and nearer, and yet it seemed as if they dared not
break upon that placid face. Another and another
rolled along, and lifted her fair, flaxen ringlets,

which floated for a moment, and then rested on the sand. After some time, a gurgling sound escaped her lips ; her eyes, that had seemed fixed in their sockets, slightly moved ; there was a quiver of the lids ; another heavy sigh, and then the lips parted. Life was returning ; and at this moment a wave lapped her cheeks, and she started as if from sleep. She stared wildly, and endeavoured to rise. As the mind recovered its consciousness, a bewildering sense of danger came over her ; tears gushed from her eyes before her tongue could utter a syllable of prayer ; and that horrible apprehension of a virtuous heart almost maddened her, while it produced the revulsion of feeling which was necessary to her immediate recovery.

" But where was her enemy ?" she asked, mentally, as she crawled out of the reach of the waves towards the cavern. " Was he still lurking by ? No, that was not probable ; yet, how could he have escaped ? Was it a dream ? No, no." And she clasped her hands and prayed for deliverance. How long she had been there, she knew not. The tide was receding. But where was he who had attacked her? As she wondered, almost fearing to breathe, she heard a sound, as of something upon the cliff above; creeping softly from her retreat, she glanced along the broad and high surface of chalk that glistened in the moonlight like a gigantic iceberg. Presently her eye rested upon a dark object that was carefully and with great difficulty climbing up that dangerous precipice. A momentary shudder passed through her; the sight was dreadful. The climber seemed to cling to the rocks with his fingers, while his feet had scarcely an inch to rest upon. If that were her enemy, there was little danger to be apprehended; for descent was impossible, unless he fell mangled and crushed upon the beach. The scene was too exciting to turn from, and though the unhappy girl trembled with cold and fright, and was exhausted with the shock which her delicate frame had sustained, she stood as it were, rooted to the spot, and her eyes were fascinated by the scene.

Still higher, there was a ledge of rock at the foot of some half-dozen steps that looked as though they had been cut in the chalky wall at some remote period; but before these could be reached, a portion of overhanging cliff had to be climbed, and this was, perhaps, the most dangerous of all. Two or three projections like flints were all that the hands could grasp, and if one of these should give way, the adventurous climber must be precipitated to the bottom of the cliff. As the man reached this point, he looked up; a heavy breath, as if the poor wretch despaired, was distinctly audible. Strange, that at that moment she prayed for his safety.

Having rested awhile, the "bold, bad man" reached the first projection; the moon shone upon his dark figure, and even his face, with its black beard, was visible. Lizzy saw his arm extended in the upward direction; he was clinging to the projection, his foot felt about for its resting place, but the point on which it found support was not visible.   He rose another inch, and then another; but the suspense was too awful—the heart sickened, and the unhappy girl at last turned away, and proceeded slowly, as the flood subsided, towards the cottage.   Presently, as she listened for every sound that might bring her hope of succour, the thud of an oar reach her ear. Then all was silent: the lashing waves rolled with their loud, and as it seemed, increasing uproar; but as she gazed across the glistening foam, the sound came once more.   It was now certain that some one approached, and she perceived a small dark object far away over that long line of foam.   Could it be the old man who was in search for her?   Heaven send it might be!   Too weak to proceed further without resting, she sank down against the cliff, and with the intense earnestness of one who listens for the footstep of a deliverer, endeavoured to persuade herself that the dark spot that now rose upon the distant wave and now sunk between the billows, was the old man's boat. It was after some time of anxious watching, that the hope of succour triumphed over her many fears; and at last she beheld the form of the old man as he struggled through the waves, and looked anxiously along the beach. Instantly Lizzy endeavoured to make him aware of her presence by waving a handker-chief, but as it was of the same hue with the chalky cliff, it was some time before the signal caught the old man's eye. At length it was seen, and he pulled for the shore. As the poor girl clasped his hand and fell upon his bosom, the relief from so great danger, produced a sensation of joy, that for awhile prevented utter-ance, and left her almost as helpless as when she lay upon the beach in the power of her enemy. Tears streamed from her eyes, and she sobbed in the fulness of immeasurable joy.

END OF VOL. II.

T. C. NEWBY, 30, Welbeck Street, Cavendish Square, London.